Gene Wolfe
14 Articles on His Fiction

MICHAEL ANDRE-DRIUSSI

ISBN: 1947614010
ISBN-13: 978-1-947614-01-7

****

"A Closer Look at the Brown Book" originally appeared in *The New York Review of Science Fiction No. 54*, February 1993.

"Gene Wolfe at the Lake of Birds" originally appeared in *Foundation No. 66*, Spring 1996.

"Posthistory 101" originally appeared in *Extrapolation Vol. 37, No. 2*, Summer 1996.

"Naming the Star of *The Fifth Head of Cerberus*" originally appeared in the chapbook *Cicerone Sinister*, published by Sirius Fiction in 2001.

"Lions and Tigers and Bears . . . of the New Sun" originally appeared online at Ultan's Library, Dec 2003.

"Gene Wolfe: the Man and His Work" originally appeared in *The Magazine of Fantasy & Science Fiction*, Apr 2007.

"The Death of Catherine the Weal and Other Stories (1992)" originally appeared online at Ultan's Library, Aug 2008.

"Gene Wolfe's Novels and *The Book of the Long Sun*" originally appeared as an introduction for the Romanian edition of *Nightside the Long Sun*, 2008.

"Japanese Lexicon for the New Sun" originally appeared online at Ultan's Library, May 2009.

"What Gene Wolfe Expects of His Readers" originally appeared online at *The Internet Review of Science Fiction*, Apr 2009.

Review of *Nightside the Long Sun* for *Quantum No. 43/44*, spring/summer 1993.

Review of *In Green's Jungles* for *The New York Review of Science Fiction No. 145*, Sep 2000.

Review of *Strange Travelers* for Ultan's Library, May 2000.

Review of *Shadows of the New Sun* for *The New York Review of Science Fiction No. 307*, Mar 2014.

CONTENTS

A CLOSER LOOK AT THE BROWN
BOOK

The Book of Wonders of Urth and Sky is perhaps the most referred-to book within Gene Wolfe's *The Book of the New Sun* and *The Urth of the New Sun* (the only other contender being Canog's *Book of the New Sun*) and some readers feel that its stories are digressive padding that serves only to slow down Severian's narrative. The "brown book," as Severian quickly comes to call it, is a collection of ancient legends obscured by time, the most interesting of which to Master Ultan is the legend of the Historians, "'which tells of a time in which every legend could be traced to half-forgotten fact. You see the paradox, I assume. Did the legend itself exist at that time? And if not, how came it into existence?'" (I, 64). Yet when Severian first opens the book, he reads "'. . . by which means a picture might be graven with such skill that the whole of it, should it be destroyed, might be recreated from a small part, and that small part be any part'" (I, 65). This describes a hologram, and is thus a verifiable bit of truth in a book of mythological odds and ends. So the brown book is full of myths underlain with history, a tug of war between legend and half-forgotten fact, or between the soft sciences of psychology and history.

One can approach myth from at least two directions, psychological or historical. To the scholar with a psychological orientation, like Joseph Campbell, mythic types are universal to man, prehistoric in origin (i.e., non-historical), and shaped by events that are both pivotal and long forgotten (discovering fire, domesticating animals, et cetera). The danger of such a global outlook is that of becoming so diffuse that, for example, everything is a "solar myth": Buddha, Odin, Achilles, St. Sebastian, even the mayor of your town, all solar myths.

Campbell avoids this failing, and in fact offers convincing evidence that all the world's myths share key elements which constitute a Jungian "collective unconscious." Wolfe has a firm grasp on this Worldwide Mythology, daring to mix such diverse gods as Abaia (Oceania), Erebus (Greek), Oannes (Babylonian), and Jurupari (South American Indians) where scholars might balk and lesser writers fail horribly.

On the other hand, for the scholar with a historic outlook like Robert Graves, myths very often refer to specific events in the history of a tribe, and so tell the group's history. Graves is so bound to historical events and speculative theories (especially those revolving around the White Goddess) that some consider him merely a sophisticated von Däniken, yet his notion of the five-part life of the sacred hero is compelling: Birth (unusual birth and childhood of the hero), Initiation (usually chthonic in nature), Reign (hero becomes king), Repose (hero does his kingly deeds, killing monsters), and Death (hero dies).

The tales of the brown book are all literary constructions, yet they play off on the tensions between fiction and fact, and they often incorporate the five-part life of the sacred hero. Furthermore, each tale from the brown book is a hologram-like representation of the entire

Book and *Urth,* compact and concentrated, but never discursive.

The Tale of the Student and His Son

We begin this inquiry with a tip-off from the 1986 essay of John Clute (*Strokes,* p. 171), wherein Wolfe himself alludes to the punning transformation of "Theseus and the Minotaur" into "Thesis and the Monitor" in "The Tale of the Student and His Son" (II, 142–159). While Clute gives the answer in a nutshell, the clues bear looking into, so in dealing with these stories we must watch for the mythic hook (in this case, Theseus), the historical hook (the Monitor), and the pun that transforms.

"The Student and His Son" is a five-part story. After a great deal of procrastination in "The Redoubt of the Magicians," the Student pens the words to create his Son. In "The Fleshing of the Hero," the Student initiates his new Son into the mystery of the Corn Maidens and the naviscaput that receives them as tribute. In the third section, "The Encounter with the Princess," the Son adds armor to a ship that he renames *Land of Virgins,* then sails off to meet Princess Noctua, who gives him the secret to killing her father and a clue to navigating his watery maze. Empowered by the goddess/princess, the Son slays the monster in "The Battle with the Ogre" by using tar smoke. Finally, in "The Death of the Student," the Student sees the ship's sails (blackened by tar smoke) and, fearing that his son had been slain, dies of grief.

As "Theseus and the Minotaur" plays a part in this story, a review of that myth is in order, using Graves's five-part life of the hero as a scaffold:

1) Birth: King Aegeus of Athens has no son by either of his two wives, and when he consults the Oracle about this he is warned not to unloosen his wineskin until he reaches home or he will die of grief. In spite of this cryptic warning, he wakes up with a hangover in Aethra's bed in

3

Troezan. Theseus is born out of wedlock and raised by his mother. (Aegeus's inability to engender offspring becomes the Student's inability to conceive of his masterwork.)

2) Initiation: Theseus is sent in his teens to meet his father Aegeus in Athens. He learns the mystery of the Minotaur and the tribute of Athenian youth sent to him, a practice Theseus vows to stop by killing the monster, whereupon Aegeus gives him a white sail to raise upon returning victorious. (Theseus first appears to Aegeus as a teenager, just as the Son appears to the Student.)

3) Reign: sailing to Crete, he meets the princess Ariadne, who offers to help him kill her half-brother the Minotaur, gives him a magic ball of thread, and instructs him on how to enter and leave the Labyrinth. This is where the sacred marriage so crucial to myth takes place, and Theseus becomes, in effect, a sacred king because of his bond to the holy and royal princess.

4) Repose: Theseus is now able to kill the Minotaur, after which he successfully fights a sea battle before escaping Crete. Unfortunately he forgets to raise the white sail. (For the Student's Son, the sea battle and slaying of the monster are merged into one.)

5) Death: Aegeus throws himself into the sea at the sight of the black sail, thinking that his only son has been killed. Somebody must die in this section, either the sacred king or, as in this case, his "tanist" substitute. (Jonas is familiar with this version of the story, as he points out to Severian "'the hero had told the king, his father, that if he failed he would return to Athens with black sails'" [II, 160].)

It is clear that "The Student and His Son" is structurally based on "Theseus and the Minotaur," but there are many details that seem cut from a different cloth: the guns, engine, paddle-wheels, and armor-plated sides of the *Land of Virgins,* as well as the naviscaput itself, the visible portion of which is described as "a long hull of narrow beam, with a single castle of iron amidships and a single gun . . . thrusting from its one embrasure" (II, 153). This is the stuff of history, in particular the battle of the *Monitor* and the *Merrimack,* the first battle between ironclads. At the beginning of the War Between the States, Union forces scuttled the powerful steam frigate *Merrimack* when they abandoned the Norfolk Navy Yard at Portsmouth, Virginia. The Confederates raised the *Merrimack,* converted it into an ironclad with several cannon on port and starboard sides, and renamed it the *Virginia* (which might be translated as "Land of Virgins"). On March 9, 1862, the *Virginia* engaged the Union ironclad *Monitor* (which had two canon in a rotating turret) in a four-hour close-range duel, which resulted in a draw. In April the *Virginia* again challenged the *Monitor,* but the challenge was refused. In May, her captain destroyed the *Virginia* as the Confederates were forced to abandon Norfolk, and in December the *Monitor* floundered and sank in heavy seas. Despite the inconclusive nature of their battle, the event marked a revolution in naval warfare.

The pun "Thesis and the Monitor" shows the confluence of "Theseus and the Minotaur," "The *Monitor* and the *Merrimack,*" and "The Student and his Thesis." In regard to solar imagery and Severian's narrative, "The Student and His Son" is also a compressed version of *The Book* and *Urth,* with Severian (the "original") playing the part of the Student, Severian (the "avatar") playing the part of the New Sun, and the old Autarch as the naviscaput/minotaur at the heart of the maze, against a backdrop of war between the north and south.

The Tale of the Boy Called Frog

Next we look at "The Tale of the Boy Called Frog," a four part story (III, 147–157). In "Early Summer and Her Son" a queen beyond the shores of Urth conceives of a son by way of a rose and names him Spring Wind. He grows up into an accomplished agriculturist and soldier, and in his travels to Urth meets a woman named Bird of the Wood, whose uncle had forced her to become a virgin priestess. As a result of this encounter, Bird of the Wood gives birth to twin sons who are immediately set out on the river in a basket.

The twins are adopted by sisters and separated in "How Frog Found a New Mother"; the one taken by the herdsman's wife is named Fish, while the other, taken by the woodcutter's wife, is named Frog. A year passes, and on the night Frog speaks his first words ("'Red flower,'" his name for fire) a saber-tooth tiger attacks the family campsite and Frog finds refuge in a wolves' den. The sabertooth (a.k.a. the Butcher), backed by the hyena, demands that Frog be given to him to eat, but the wolves refuse, adopting Frog as their own. The Senate of Wolves officially accepts Frog over the objection of the sabertooth in "The Black Killer's Gold," largely due to the vote of the Naked One, teacher of the young wolves, and the ransom in gold paid by the Panther. In "The Plowing of the Fish" Frog takes control of the animal kingdom by his mastery of fire. The twins are reunited, and they divide their legacy such that Fish gets the city and farmlands and Frog gets the wild hills. The human population of Frog's kingdom grows, and they steal women from other people, until Frog decides that they need a city of their own, so he takes a white cow and bull from Fish's herds, harnesses them to a plow, and plows a furrow to mark the future wall. When Fish sees the furrow, he laughs and jumps over it, and Frog's people kill him for doing so. Frog has Fish buried in the furrow to assure the fertility of the land, a technique he learned from Squanto, the Naked One.

"The Boy Called Frog" seems to be based upon the story of Romulus and Remus, legendary founders of Rome. Again, applying the five-part pattern:

1) Birth: Juno (who gives her name to June, a month in 'early summer') is impregnated by a flower and gives birth to Mars (who gives his name to March, a month known

for its 'spring wind'). Mars grows up as an agricultural god, but then takes up arms and becomes a soldier god (this is one of the distinctions between him and Ares the Greek god of war). Mars dallies with Rhea Silvanus ('bird of the wood') and she has the twins Romulus and Remus, whom she must set adrift on the river.

2) Initiation: Romulus and Remus are suckled by a she-wolf, and then adopted by the herdsman Faustulus and his wife Acca Larentia. Frog and Fish are raised separately.

3) Reign: the twins inherit the kingdom. This occurs in the fourth section of "The Boy Called Frog."

4) Repose: Remus jumps over the half-built wall of Romulus's new city and is killed for doing so. Romulus creates a senate of one hundred senators, whose descendents would be called patricians, and leads the capture of the Sabine women. All of these elements recur in "Frog," though the order is a bit scrambled: Frog's people steal women before they kill Fish, not after. The senate of Wolves appears in the second section.

5) Death: Romulus dies and is deified as Quirinus. The four-part structure of "Frog" is a truncation of an implied five-part structure, paralleling "Student" as well as *Book* and *Urth*. This technique of abruptly cutting off the story is nowhere better illustrated than in the performance of Dr. Talos' five-act play, "Eschatology and Genesis." We see four acts of eschatology, but the last act (that of genesis) is never played out for the audience, perhaps because Baldanders is an enemy of the New Sun and cannot bear to see him triumph, even in play.

The direct correspondence between "Frog" and "Romulus and Remus" is not so rigorous as that between "The Student and His Son" and "Theseus and the Minotaur." The narrative style takes on some of the characteristics of American Indian legends, where animals are essentially humanoid: the Wolf fingers his sword; the Butcher, by clues a saber-tooth tiger, is said to fight with two daggers; the She-wolf wears a skirt. The separation of the twins, the host of animal characters, and the Senate of Wolves all form another thread, one that leads to the Jungle Books of Rudyard Kipling.

"Mowgli's Brothers" fits "Frog" like a glove, filling in the sections that do not fit the legend of Romulus and Remus. It opens with the wolf couple in their burrow with four cubs. They hear the sound of the Tiger (compare "it was the noise that bewilders woodcutters and gypsies sleeping in the open, and makes them run sometimes into the very mouth of the tiger" with the similar line in "Frog") and then the boy crawls into their den. The Tiger and the Jackal demand that the boy be given to them, but the wolves refuse. The she-wolf names the boy "Mowgli," meaning "Frog." At the Wolf Pack at the Council Rock, the wolf-couple ask that Mowgli be recognized as a wolf. The Tiger restates his claim, but is countered by the vote of Baloo the bear and the ransom of a killed bull paid by Bagheera the panther. Mowgli refers to fire as "Red Flower," which the animals fear.

So the mythic hook of "Frog" is double: the legend of Romulus and Remus fused with the feral child tales of Kipling. (Do you balk at my reference to "Mowgli's Brothers" as mythic? I should trace the "wild man" motif back to the Epic of Gilgamesh.) When Frog and Fish divide up their heritage there is a trace of the Sumerian Gilgamesh (the king) and Enkidu (the wild-man), and the biblical Cain (the farmer) and Abel (the nomad), but both models are inverted when Frog (Enkidu/Abel) kills Fish (Gilgamesh/Cain). The unresolved details cluster around the character of the Naked One, whose role in "Mowgli's Brothers" is taken by Baloo the bear. But a bear would hardly be called "the naked one," and the character in question is also known as the Savage and "Squanto." Which leads to the historical stratum.

Squanto was a North American Indian of the Pawtuxet tribe, kidnapped in 1615 by an English captain. He lived in England for four years, then returned to North America, where he acted as an interpreter in concluding a treaty between the Pilgrim settlers and Massasoit in 1621 (the source, perhaps, of the Naked One's vote to recognize Frog as a wolf). Squanto became friendly with the Plymouth colonists, and is known for helping them with their fishing and planting (parallel to the same in "Frog"). He contracted smallpox and died in 1622 while acting as a guide and interpreter.

The historical thread leads us to the first Thanksgiving Day in Plymouth Colony, 1621. Other details seem to confirm the American setting: the Senate of Wolves (not Kipling's "Wolf Pack") is led by a President; Bagheera, the panther of the Jungle Books, has escaped from captivity and bears the mark of a collar, recalling the slavery practiced in the United States — honed by the existence of the "Black Panthers" of the 1960s and the fact that in "Frog" the Black Killer pays the ransom for Frog's freedom in gold rather than a slain bull. Other correspondences are simply curious: Early Summer conceived of Spring Wind by a rose, and the *Mayflower* which brought the Pilgrims was named after the hawthorn, a type of rose; the fratricide of Fish might be another reference to the War Between the States; and the "woodcutter" who adopted Frog may be a mask for John Carver (died 1621), the first governor of Plymouth Colony.

Perhaps the pun-that-transforms would be "Romulus and Uncle Remus," remembering that the Uncle Remus stories by Joel Chandler Harris also featured anthropomorphic animals as characters. Considering *The Book* as an expanded version of "Frog," Severian plays the part of Frog, the Old Autarch takes the part of Fish, the ritual sacrifice, and the "city" Frog will build is none other than Ushas, the Urth of the New Sun. And the war against the Other Lords is a war against slavery, as the intent of Abaia, Erebus, and the others is not to destroy the inhabitants of Urth but to enslave them.

The Shorter Tales in Brief

Of course, not all of the stories in the brown book are made up of five distinct parts, nor are the various hooks (where they exist) always so deeply encrypted. "The Boy Who Hooked the Sun" (*Weird Tales,* Spring 1988), for example, is ostensibly set on the emerald-studded coast of Atlantis, where a boy (whose father trades with the barbarians of Hellas) hooks the sun while fishing and several people try to talk him into letting it go (the richest man, the strongest man, the cleverest man, the magic woman, the most foolish man) before he finally does so at the urging of his mother, but even then, he reasons "the time must come when I live and she does not; and when that time comes, surely I will bait my hook again" (*WT,* p. 22). The boy obviously resembles Severian dragging the New Sun across space, the others are perhaps Vodalus, Baldanders, Typhon, the Cumaean, (no guess for "most foolish"), Earth as the mother, and Urth as the dead mother. The structure is seven-part, suggesting the seven planetary bodies of the week, but otherwise the history and mythology seem right up front in the form of "Atlantis" and "Hellas."

"The Town that Forgot Fauna" (*Urth,* p. 232) tells of nine men who travel up a river "when the plow was new," searching for a site to build a new city. They find an old woman with a garden and try to buy her land with copper, silver, and lastly gold. She finally agrees on the condition that they keep a garden in the center of the city, and erect a statue of the woman in precious material. They keep their promise with a small garden and a statue of painted wood, but years later a merchant buys the plot and burns the statue. Before long the town became a ghost town, uninhabited save for one old woman who keeps a garden at its center. Again, the mythology is right up front: the old woman is Fauna, also known as Mother Nature. "When the plow was new" points to Triptolemos, who, according to Greek myth, invented the plow and (quite significantly) started the Eleusinian rites of Demeter, the Great Mother Goddess. The nine men are a cipher, and might be the Nine Worthies (Joshua, David, and Judas Maccabaeus; Hector, Alexander, and Julius Caesar; Arthur, Charlemagne, and Godfrey of Bouillon), but it is difficult to be conclusive. As for American history, the buying of land smacks of the purchase of Manhattan Island for trinkets, and the existence of Central Park strengthens the allusion. (The Statue of Liberty might stand-in for the statue of Fauna.) Unmistakably this is a story about the resiliency of Mother Nature, and marks the transformation of Earth into Urth, and Urth into Ushas.

Empires of Foliage and Flower

Published only in hardcover by Cheap Street, *Empires of Foliage and Flower* is both the longest story from the brown book and the most difficult to come by. It is a story of two empires at war, one Yellow, the other Green, and its main characters are an eremite called Father Thyme and a female of variable age known only as the child. The text of *Empires* is composed of ten unnamed sections, and the story covers a period of six days (objectively speaking).

1) Thyme meets the child, an infant playing with peas as soldiers, and takes her along with him in search of peace. As they walk west, they both age dramatically.

2) The next day they continue west to Vert, capital of the Green Empire. The child is now a young woman.

3) Prince Patizithes, enamored of the child, arranges for her to meet the Green Emperor, and then seduces her.

4) On the third day the child is given a green dress for her meeting with the Emperor. The meeting goes badly, but when a general asks Thyme how to win the war, Thyme answers, "'You may win . . . when your army is dressed in yellow.'"

5) Thyme and the child continue west, into the

mountain range. She gives birth before dawn in a bush near a battlefield. She names her son Barrus, after her brother. A passing soldier gives her his gray cloak, which had once been green.

6) As they continue through the mountains, they watch a battle at a distant pass.

7) They camp that night near the enemy army.

8) Barrus walks with them during the fourth day. They arrive at Zanth, capital of the Yellow Empire, and meet a meager man who leads them to lodging. This man turns out to be the Yellow Emperor, who rarely sleeps in the palace due to the threat of assassination. The Emperor holds teenager Barrus as hostage, and says that if he proves faithful, he may wind up on the throne of a conquered Vert. Thyme tells the Emperor how to win, then leaves the city on the fifth morning, heading east with the child.

9) At a mountain pass the travelers find yellow flowered vines choking the trees they climb. The vines sprout from the skeletal remains of green soldiers, and green moss grows on the bones of yellow soldiers. Thyme says, "'During the long years in which I have ringed Urth, I have seen that the more nation differs from nation, the more difficult it is for one to trust another. Thus I advised each empire to make itself more like its foe. Alas, they were too much alike already. Each saw my advice not as a road to peace but as a ruse to win'" to which the girl adds, "'And now the laurels war with the vines.'"

10) They come again to Vert where they see "soldiers in argent armor standing guard at its gates, and a silver flag flying above the battlements." The child dwindles to an infant, and Thyme leaves her in the yard he had found her in.

It is not difficult to see how these ten sections collapse into the five-part pattern of the hero: the first two give the unusual childhood of the child; the next two give her initiation into sexuality (where she wears "a green gown as any virgin nymph" might wear); sections five and six find her in her reign as mother in gray; in seven and eight she is a tired crone in the Yellow city; and in the last two she is returned to infancy, with the Green Emperor (if not both emperors) dying in her place as tanists, or more properly, dying for her, as the child has become an aspect of the Great Goddess.

As for its mythic level, the title brings to mind the Celtic "Battle of the Trees," a poem about the fight between the forces of Light (trees) and Death (serpents), but this does not seem to correspond to *Empires*. The motif of green and yellow points to the seasonal shift from Spring to Autumn, and the constant reference to plants ("Thyme" who is a "sage"; "peas" confused with "peace"; et cetera) reinforces this notion, so at one level the war is the natural vegetative growth cycle. It is also about the warlike nature of all life, even plants themselves, with the implication that as a higher life form, *Homo sapiens* has the ability to stop the fighting. That is to say, Nature is cruel. This cruelty goes further than the species-versus-species variety, descending to the battle of the sexes: recall Master Ash in the Last House, a figure from Norse mythology (the first man, carved from a tree) where he is paired with a wife named Vine. Very depressing, to have Adam and Eve killing each other before they even get out of the garden. (Master Ash also comes to mind with regard to Thyme's habit of growing young or old as he walks, for when Severian first hears the tread of Ash it sounds to him like that of an old or sick man, but as Ash comes closer his steps become firmer and more swift.)

A hint of Jack Vance's "Ulan Dhor" is present as well, a story from *The Dying Earth* that features a city torn by centuries of civil war between two factions, the Green and the Gray.

> "Five thousand years and the wretches still quarrel? Time has taught them no wisdom! Then stronger agencies must be used . . . Behold!". . . . The

> tentacles sprouted a thousand appendages . . . These ranged the city, and wherever there was crumbling or mark of age the tentacles dug, tore, blasted, burnt; then spewed new materials into place (Vance, *The Dying Earth*, p. 104).

The reconstruction of the city by its awakened immortal in "Ulan Dhor" is echoed by the resurrection of the Stone Town by its god Apu Punchau, which happens in *The Claw of the Conciliator* soon after the conversation between Severian and the Cumaean about *Empires*.

Chinese legend includes a character named the Yellow Emperor, originally known as Huangti, the third of the Three Kings of ancient China, inventor of pottery and houses. Around 2600 B.C., Huangti's people settled the "loess," a land of fertile ground around the Yellow River, but before long, encroaching neighbors (led by Ch'ih Yu, who called himself the Red Emperor and worshiped the gods of Fire) caused Huangti to fight the first war. He crushed Ch'ih Yu and took the entire loess, then all the other tribes hailed him as lord. He moved his capital to Pingyang, central to the tribal lands, and ruled as the Yellow Emperor. Among other marvelous things, the Yellow Emperor is credited with winning the war against the mirror people who invaded Earth one night, imprisoning them and forcing them to slavishly mimic all the actions of men.

This looks promising. We have a mythic hook for the Yellow Emperor, and the mysterious empire of silver (which would be the color for mirror people). Ascian soldiers wear "silvery caps and shirts in place of armor" (IV, 208), and the magic mirrors of Urth represent the highest technology, portals to and from the higher universe of Yesod, if not other universes as well. But what about the Green Empire? The fact that emeralds are the currency of the empire calls to mind the Emerald City of Oz, but goes no further. For the Green Empire we must turn at last to history.

"Patizithes" is an unusual name in the Urth Cycle, where characters are named after saints (if they are on the side of the New Sun) or mythological figures (usually enemies of the New Sun) or both (in a few ambiguous cases), for Patizithes is, in fact, the name of a historical figure who was neither saint nor myth. In the ancient Middle East, Patizithes was a Median magus left in charge of Cambyses' household when the latter went on his campaign against Egypt. Patizithes plotted revolt against Cambyses and carried it out in 525 B.C. by setting his brother Gaumata on the throne under the name of Smerdis. In 521 B.C. Darius killed Gaumata and founded the Persian Empire.

This Middle Eastern connection is alluded to in *Empires* by one of the prince's many titles: Margrave of the Magitae. (The Magitae were the people of Arabia Felix, or modern Yemen.) Following our historical hook, we must ask: if the Green Empire is Persia, then against whom do they war? The Persian Wars (500–479) were fought against the Greeks to a relative stalemate (similar to the war between the Green and the Yellow), but it is hard to imagine the independent city-states of ancient Greece being called an empire. A more likely candidate is the empire of Alexander (334–323), which conquered all of the Persian Empire before itself collapsing when Alexander died. From a historical standpoint Alexander's campaign was a continuation of the Greco-Persian struggle, which ended, as in *Empires,* with both nations destroyed.

There are a few curious references within the text that may act as a sort of carbon-dating for *Empires,* to wit: "though long lives might pass like a night and the New Sun sunder the centuries" and later, the good soldier says, "'By the book! . . . What in the name of awful Abaia are you two up to?'" None of the other brown book stories ever make reference to the New Sun, a concept dating to the era of Typhon at the end of the Age of the Monarch.

"Frog" refers at points to the Pancreator, and while the naviscaput may allude to Abaia that name is never mentioned. All the other stories are firmly rooted in the Age of Myth (that is, our own history), but the brown book was published three or four centuries before Severian's era (thus, by my calculations, around the seventh century of the Age of the Autarch), so it appear that the action in *Empires* takes place sometime after the era of Typhon, yet long enough before the printing of the brown book to become properly obscured by the passage of time. (One might argue that the text of the brown book has been corrupted by editors adding current theological references to old legends, which is a possibility. But since no other section, even the various fragments, ever mentions Abaia or the New Sun, there is little to substantiate the notion of theological corruption.) The posthistoric event that seems to be commemorated is the cataclysmic second invasion of the mirror people, the arrival and entrenchment of the Other Lords, and the transformation of the Green and Yellow Empires into Ascia.

Empires reflects *The Book* and *Urth* in a number of ways; initially as an apocalyptic struggle that stretches on for generations and has no good or bad side, just a murky middle. Recall that the Ascians are not merely tools of evil, but want mankind to return to the stars as masters, and recall as well those sailors who valiantly fight against the death of Urth in the Hall of Justice on Yesod. It also points to the trials of transformation and eventual rebirth, not only for Urth but for Severian as well. And last but not least looms the five-part pattern.

The Five Parts of the New Sun

Zooming from micro to macro, consider *The Book* and *Urth* as stages of the sacred hero's life.

1) Birth: Severian is born at least two times in *The*

Shadow of the Torturer, first by Catherine in her cell, then again years later by the undine Juturna who rescues him from drowning. In comic book terms, this second birth is the part where little Sev, drowning in the river, utters the magic word "SHAZAM!" and turns into Severman, able to walk the corridors of time (eventually, at least). The Severian who comes out of the river is not the same Severian that went into the river; somebody died, someone else was reborn.

2) Initiation: in *The Claw of the Conciliator,* Severian is initiated into the cannibalistic ritual of the Vodalarii. As we have seen, the initiation stage is typically about the mysteries of life and death; in "Student" the focus was on the ripening and harvest of man (or "Corn Maidens") as well as grain; the mysteries of birth are examined as Frog is adopted into a secret society, and initiated in their customs. What mysteries of life and death could possibly exist for journeyman Severian, who was adopted by the torturers, raised amid incredible pain and suffering, and taught the scientific techniques of excruciation, except that of experiencing as his own the life and death of another through the analeptic alzabo?

3) Reign: Severian ascends the mountain and begins his trials in *The Sword of the Lictor.* He is stripped of all external trappings: his companion Dorcas, his sword *Terminus Est,* his relic the *Claw.* His sacred marriage (such as it is) with the widow (in mythic terms, she might be called "Isis") gives him an instant family, but most of them are quickly stripped away. (Does the phrase "Who will help the Widow's Son?" ring any bells? Cause Masonic feelers to quiver, or hackles to rise?) Little Severian, his newly adopted son and childhood self (call him "Severboy") in a pastoral world he never knew, is vaporized in an instant. And through it all, Severian becomes master of himself, servant no longer to any person or institution, such that when he identifies himself as "Grand Master Severian" to the villagers of Lake Diuturna, he is not telling a simple lie,

but one that masks a deeper truth.

4) Repose: in *The Citadel of the Autarch,* Severian goes through the horrific mass combat of war, kills and consumes the minotaur/sacrifice, the Old Autarch, and prepares for the final journey. Some readers may balk at this depiction of the Old Autarch as Ogre, offering Baldanders as the most Ogre-like character on Urth. Here is conclusive evidence linking the minotaur to the Old Autarch, from a scene where Severian slips into the Corridors of Time while looking at the autarch: "A man with the horns and muzzled face of a bull bent over me, a constellation sprung to life. . . . He listened intently, turning his head to watch me from one brown eye" (IV, 189-190).

5) Death: Severian dies (a few times, at least) and is reborn; Urth dies and is reborn as Ushas.

It all looks so self-evident. If I had written this before the announcement that Wolfe was writing *Urth,* it would have been a penetrating insight, but even at this late date I hope that it is not without some worth. It seems that in creating a new mythos in the New Sun, Gene Wolfe has (consciously or otherwise) incorporated not only the myths of several differing nations and times, effectively tapping into the Jungian "collective unconscious," but also the five-part pattern of the hero, a structure that shows up in the large scale as well as the small. I say "consciously or otherwise" because, as Wolfe tells it in *The Castle of the Otter, The Book* was originally meant to be a novella, then a novel, then a trilogy, before finally becoming a tetralogy, yet even then there was an implied fifth part, just like in "Frog" and "Eschatology and Genesis." But why end a tale at its fourth part? To end on the upbeat, for one, as well as to avoid the difficulties of death and first person past tense narration. It is almost as if the meme of the five-part hero was struggling to be expressed through Gene Wolfe, rather than a conscious blueprint or a happy "subconscious" coincidence. It is also possible that from the beginning Wolfe had some presentiment of his future.

****

Works Cited

Jorge Luis Borges, *The Book of Imaginary Beings,* Penguin, 1987

Joseph Campbell, *The Hero with a Thousand Faces,* Princeton, 1973

———, *Primitive Mythology,* Penguin, 1987

John Clute, *Strokes,* Serconia Press, 1988

Robert Graves, *The Greek Myths,* Penguin, 1974

Rudyard Kipling, *All the Mowgli Stories,* Doubleday, 1936

Jack Vance, *The Dying Earth,* Pocket Science Fantasy, 1977

Gene Wolfe, *The Shadow of the Torturer,* Simon and Schuster, 1980

———, *The Claw of the Conciliator,* Timescape Books, 1981

———, *The Sword of the Lictor,* Timescape Books, 1982

———, *The Citadel of the Autarch,* Timescape Books, 1983

———, *The Castle of the Otter,* Science Fiction Book Club Edition, 1982

———, *Empires of Foliage and Flower,* manuscript, 1987 (?)

———, *The Urth of the New Sun,* Tor Books, 1987

———, "The Boy Who Hooked the Sun," *Weird Tales #290,* Spring 1988

****

Afterword to "A Closer Look at the Brown Book"

This piece was published in 1993, ahead of the first edition of *Lexicon Urthus* (1994).

The use of a Science Fiction Book Club edition raises some eyebrows. At the time I was more focused on citing volume and chapter to better serve all editions. The Lexicon first edition also used SFBC, and a later chapbook had a table converting SFBC page numbers into page numbers for Simon & Schuster and Orb editions.

GENE WOLFE AT THE LAKE OF BIRDS

As everybody knows, Gene Wolfe's *Book of the New Sun* is heavily layered with symbols, each highly charged with hidden significance. The somberly baroque landscape is cluttered with curios, some grotesque and others fanciful, but even against this background of symbolic radiation some sections are so highly charged that one's hair begins to stand on end.

These supercharged areas undoubtedly mark very important spots for readers to take note (at various levels) and for treasure hunters to dig. The three chapters (ch. 22-24) of *The Shadow of the Torturer* dealing with the Lake of Birds is one of these supercharged sections — the preceding chapters introducing the Botanical Gardens of Nessus set the pace by cranking up the dream-like quality by several degrees.

But before we get to the Lake of Birds, a very brief gloss on books outside and inside *TBNS*.

The main narrative thread of *TBNS* is something like the *Great Expectations* of *I, Claudius* on *The Dying Earth*. That is to say, Jack Vance's *Dying Earth* provides the landscape; *I, Claudius* by Robert Graves gives the political and religious structure, as well as the whole "backing into the throne" theme; and Charles Dickens' *Great Expectations* adds the bildungsroman and the hidden family relationships. There is, of course, a lot of detail work tracing from Borges: *The Book of Imaginary Beings* with its collection of creatures; the story "Funes the Memorious," whose hero has a photographic memory not unlike Severian's; the story "Library of Babel," so similar to the Library of Nessus; and so on, into seemingly infinite regression.

But setting aside outside sources for the moment, there are two works within *TBNS* that seem to be blueprints for the whole: one is the fabled brown book; the other is the play "Eschatology and Genesis." I have already written an essay on the brown book (*NYRSF* #54, Feb. 1993) and I may yet write one on the play, but here they are in a nutshell:

The brown book offers stories that contain the five-fold pattern of the hero's life, a structure written about by Robert Graves in *The White Goddess*. Those five stages are: (1) Birth, (2) Initiation, (3) Reign, (4) Repose, and (5) Death. The main stories of the brown book presented in *TBNS* ("The Tale of the Student and His Son" and "The Tale of the Boy Called Frog") have this structure, and for Severian himself these stages are each covered in the five volumes of his narrative.

The play "Eschatology and Genesis" is trickier. As the title suggests, it deals with the transition from one creation period to the next, a mixing of endings and beginnings. As a result, the Armageddon of the old creation is simultaneously the Eden of the new: the graveyard of death is also a garden of birth. In vanilla-Christian terms, the main characters of the play are Adam, Eve, the Serpent (Demiurge or pretender to the throne), and Lilith (the first Eve and/or consort to the Demiurge). These characters must battle to determine the fate of the new creation.

That's enough for now. Just remember the graveyard/garden bit, and the characters.

Now we are back on the main trail, the Lake of Birds is just around the next corner. But before we get there, just one more tangent, a very brief gloss on themes and threads leading to those three chapters in *The Shadow of the Torturer*.

We begin *The Book of the New Sun* with scenes and scenarios from Dickens' *Great Expectations* — Severian is like Pip, drawn from a graveyard into helping a criminal; Thecla is one version of Estella (the higher class girl he expects to marry), Agia is another (the more vicious Estella); Valeria is Biddy (the same class girl Pip should marry); the grounded starships forming the Citadel of the Autarch, referred to as "hulks" in *Urth of the New Sun*, echo the prison-ship hulks of *Great Expectations*. And in the course of this version, Pip will marry Biddy in the end.

Agia as the more vicious Estella, indeed! She is one of the most powerful characters in *TBNS*, and her story reads like something out of a Quentin Tarantino movie. Consider:

One morning while she was opening up the rag shop, Agia saw Severian approaching and assumed that he was an armiger in costume for a party. Her merchant senses told her that both his costume and his sword were far more elaborate than most (perhaps historical relics), and her streetwise senses told her that he was in unfamiliar territory. She probably thought he was a newly arrived armiger from the provinces.

In any event, she and her twin brother Agilus quickly set up their pattern for a con job meant to fleece the naive of their heirlooms: as Agilus bargained over the cloak and sword, Agia donned the armor of a Septentrion Guard, entered the store and delivered the challenge to a duel with averns at the Sanguinary Field. They hoped that Severian would be so frightened that he would sell the cloak and sword for a small fraction of their real value. (They had done such things before, albeit for much smaller stakes.)

The plan began to go awry, however. Severian accepted the challenge, even though he didn't understand it (he assumed that it had something to do with Thecla). Agia tried again to scare him off by getting them into a reckless fiacre race, which ended when their cab crashed into the tent-cathedral of the Pelerines. Again, Agia was quick to size-up the situation and seize the opportunity by stealing the priceless Claw of the Conciliator from the ruined altar. She planted it in Severian's sabretache without him knowing.

This gem was enough to buy a palace. Suddenly the con-job on Severian was for a paltry sum, and besides, in the course of talking with him she had decided that he really wasn't a naive armiger from the outlands; he was in fact a professional torturer. And he seemed to have ties to Vodalus, the exultant rebel. Sensing that they were in over their heads, she began to fear for Agilus, but there was no way to contact him. Agia grew edgy and began jumping at shadows — at the Inn of Lost Loves she tried to use her sex appeal to seduce Severian and snatch back the Claw (which he still didn't know he had) but she failed. At the Sanguinary Field she shouted out Severian's name and title of torturer as a potential warning for Agilus, but it didn't work; she urged Severian to refuse the combat on a technicality, but this also failed. Agilus won the duel by cheating, but then a miracle occurred and Severian was resurrected.

As sordid and Dickensian as it is, our sprawling city is not Victorian London, it is post-historical Nessus — named after the centaur who treacherously killed the solar hero Heracles. And the river running through the narrative is not the Thames, it is the River Gyoll — the river of death from Norse mythology. Which means that we are reading about a trip through some kind of hell; which reminds us of Dante.

Dante's *Inferno* is in there, all right. If we don't suspect that Nessus, with its superabundance of death imagery and sorrow, is some form of the infernal city Dis, there's always that sign on the doorway of the worldship Yesod in

Urth of the New Sun which Gunnie reads as "No hope for those who enter here," a nice paraphrase of the inscription above the gate to Dante's Hell, but Apheta corrects Gunnie's reading as "Every hope [for those who enter here]" (ch. 23). So what one sees as hell, the other sees as heaven.

Remember: Dante is going through hell and heaven to get a rose in the end.

•

Which brings us, at long last, to the three chapters at the Lake of Birds.

"Dorcas" is the name of Chapter 22 that introduces us to the Garden of Endless Sleep. This garden has a dreary marsh, a lake (the Lake of Birds) that serves as an aquatic graveyard, and a farther shore of death that combine to form a netherworld "wasteland" (hellish imagery) that is paradoxically called a "garden" (edenic images). Severian enters this dead Eden with Agia as his guide (as Virgil stood to Dante, and in a sense as Sibyl stood to Aeneas) in order to pick up a flower to use as a weapon in a duel (another fine paradox). The quest to pick a plant reminds us of *The Aeneid* where Virgil writes of Aeneas retrieving the golden bough for a trip through Avernus to the underworld, as well as the earlier *Epic of Gilgamesh* where that hero gets the rejuvenating plant (from an island or the bottom of the sea).

Lake Avernus is a small crater lake in Southern Italy near Cuma. In ancient times its intense sulfuric vapors (caused by volcanic activity) supposedly killed the birds flying over it, hence the name "Avernus" from Greek meaning "without birds." Against this folk etymology, Robert Graves argues (*Greek Myths*, section 31.2) that the etymological root for Avernus is, like that of King Arthur's Avalon, the Indo-European *abol* meaning "apple." Phonetically there is a great similarity between Avernus and Avalon, which is only odd because one is a kind of hell, the other a kind of heaven.

Since Severian and Agia are a man and a woman alone in a garden, there is a hint of Adam and Eve to them. But since Agia is trying to trick and/or kill Severian, we can look ahead a bit and call her Lilith, the first Eve. We know that one of the models for Nessus is Byzantium, and the marvel of that city is a church called "Hagia Sophia" (meaning "Holy Wisdom"), and "Sophia" is sometimes considered a consort to God . . . but I'm getting ahead of myself. Suffice to say that as Agia has wisdom and is acting as a guide to Severian she is in a sense "Hagia Sophia" (although perhaps not quite "holy").

Along comes the unnamed boatman. Now, when doing a crossword puzzle, if one finds the question "Name of underworld boatman" the answer is usually "Charon." In Greek mythology Charon is the ferryman on the river Styx, but in Dante's *Inferno* (canto 3) he works the river Acheron (river of Sorrows) between the vestibule and Limbo, the First Circle of Hell:

> And here, advancing toward us, in a boat
> an aged man — his hair was white with years —
> was shouting: "Woe to you, corrupted souls!
>
> Forget your hope of ever seeing Heaven:
> I come to lead you to the other shore,
> to the eternal dark, to fire and frost.
>
> And you approaching there, you living soul,
> keep well away from these — they are the dead."
> But when he saw I made no move to go,
>
> he said: "Another way and other harbors —
> not here — will bring you passage to your shore:
> a lighter craft will have to carry you" (lines 79–90).

Our nameless boatman, who is revealed much later to be Severian's paternal grandfather, doesn't shout like Dante's Charon, but that detail about the boat rings as the boatman refuses to ferry Agia and Severian: "Too heavy for my little boat. There's but room for Cas and me here. You great folk would capsize us" (Ch. 22). So on the Dante track we are now in the vestibule or antechamber of Hell.

The boatman tells Severian that the dead wander in the lake, propelled by currents, but also that the dead rise and are stung back to death by the deadly avern plants. This is clearly wishful thinking on his part, since he longs to be with his wife, and it has the mythic ring to it (considering all the devices to keep the dead in their place, to maintain the separation between the worlds of the living and the dead), but it also hints that skullduggery is afoot in this placid garden. In this fantastic graveyard, murder might go unnoticed.

Our boatman's repetitive searching of the water echoes Rudesind the curator's picture cleaning of chapter 5 — both aged men are searching for objects that connect them with their own pasts, but where Rudesind is narcissistically looking for the portrait made of him as a boy, the boatman is searching for his lost love, Cas (also known as Dorcas, which is the name of the chapter). This does not sound much like Charon: rather it invokes Orpheus, who journeyed to Hades to bring back his dead wife Eurydice only to lose her again at the last instant by looking back. Dante places Orpheus in the First Circle of the *Inferno* (canto IV, line 140), and Virgil writes in his *Georgics* that at the moment when Orpheus looked back, "Three times did thunder peal over the pools of Avernus."

And our boatman *did* look back, just as Orpheus did. When his wife's body slipped under the brown waters he saw her eyes open, a vision which haunts him for the rest of his life. It seems likely that at some level he feels guilty of accidentally murdering her.

The odd thing is, Dorcas herself later has a dream with a very similar scene:

I am in a boat poled across a spectral lake. . . . It is not [Hildegrin's] boat but a much smaller one. An old man poles it, and I lie at his feet. I am awake, but I cannot move. My arm trails in the black water. Just as we are about to touch shore, I fall from the boat, but the old man does not see me, and as I sink through the water I know that he has never known I was there at all. Soon the light is gone, and I am very cold. Far above me, I hear a voice I love calling my name, but I cannot remember whose voice it is." (*Claw*, chapter 22)

In mythical terms, Dorcas dreams herself on Charon's boat, crossing the river separating the world of the living from the world of the dead. But before the boat can arrive at that far shore, she falls into the water and is lost in the limbo between worlds — half-alive and half-dead. The idea that Charon did not know she was on his boat suggests that she was not scheduled to be there, that is, she was not dead.

In detective terms ("no myths, ma'am, just the facts"), the same dream suggests that she remembers being put into the lake by her husband: and while there is a certain amount of "out of body experience" in *TBNS*, there is no evidence that the dead are capable of seeing their own funerals, this points again (perhaps tenuously) to the notion that Dorcas was not dead. Which would mean that yes, her husband did accidentally kill her. ("Book him, Danno.")

So our boatman is an Orpheus doomed to act the role of Charon, like a titan guilty of some terrible crime against the gods. The mythic picture is perfectly clear — we are in hell, simultaneously Dante's antechamber and the Greek Hades.

Suddenly the scene changes as Severian falls into the water and loses his sword. He dives deeper after it, again reminding us of Gilgamesh going to the bottom of the sea, but then something unexpected happens — at the instant that Severian grasps the sword, he also grips another hand, so that "it seemed the hand's owner was returning my property to me, like the tall mistress of the Pelerines." The lake, the lady, and the sword — this tableau comes from the Arthurian Cycle.

Add King Arthur to the mix. Hardly a surprise, is it, since Avernus is so much like Avalon. As the chapter closes, enter the Lady of the Lake, Eurydice of Hades, and Eve of Eden, all in one body known as Dorcas.

•

"Hildegrin" is the name of chapter 23.

Severian begins the chapter by coughing up water. This resonates with his near-drowning experience at the beginning of the book, where death by inhaling water and birth from expelling water are intertwined. It also ties in with the pattern of vomiting that comes just before threshold moments: in *Shadow of the Torturer,* Severian vomits on the Feast Day in chapter 11 and in the next chapter betrays his guild by giving Thecla a knife; in *Claw of the Conciliator* he vomits in chapter 10 before the feast of Vodalus, then consumes Thecla in chapter 11; in *Sword of the Lictor* Dorcas tells in chapter 10 of regurgitating the lead shot, and by the next chronological chapter (12) Severian and Dorcas have fled Thrax in opposite directions.

The waters of Hades have special properties, the most famous being Lethe, the water of forgetfulness at which the shades drink to forget their earthly lives. While forgetting is nearly impossible for Severian, the experience of swimming in the Lake of Birds does give him a certain amount of disorientation.

Switch back to Dante, who was just told that he couldn't ride the punt with Charon. After hearing the bad news, Dante swoons and wakes up in the First Circle on the other side of the river Acheron.

When Severian gathers his wits, it is almost as if he too is on a different shore — in addition to Agia, there is the nameless blonde woman (Dorcas) who helped him out of the water, and there is also "a big, beef-faced man" (who will turn out to be Hildegrin). "Beef-faced man" sounds like an allusion to the Minotaur, another figure of Greek mythology who also appears in Dante's *Inferno,* as the first guardian of the Seventh Circle of Hell. One of the first things that Hildegrin says is "Who in Phlegethon are you?" and Phlegethon is the fiery river of blood which flows through the Seventh Circle, that region reserved for those who committed violence against others.

So on the Dante track we have jumped from the antechamber to the Seventh Circle, a region of the *Inferno* which is also noteworthy as the section where the treacherous centaur Nessus appears and is forced to act as ferryman, carrying Dante and Virgil across Phlegethon. During this river passage, Dante has two guides: Virgil (the good) and Nessus (the bad). The bodies they pass among belong to terrible sinners — tyrants and murderers.

To help the wet and shivering couple, Hildegrin offers them brandy from a flask in the shape of a dog with the bone in his mouth as the stopper — a reference to the sop for Cerberus, the guardian of Hades who appears in many tales of the underworld, including Dante's *Inferno,* where Cerberus is in the Third Circle. Which sets off its own recursive loop-the-lupine loop with echoes of *The Fifth Head of Cerberus.*

That Dorcas cannot at first remember her own name points to Lethe — she has drunk of the waters of forgetfulness. Hildegrin contributes to the skullduggery theme begun by the boatman by offering a theory that Dorcas was the victim of foul play and/or a coma from which she awoke. This is the operative theory until much later when the unsuspected presence of the Claw will offer another theory; that Dorcas was truly dead until the relic resurrected her. And in the Christian tradition, Dorcas was a widow resurrected by Saint Peter.

Hildegrin has Agia sit in the bow of the boat, Severian and Dorcas in the stern, and he himself sits in the middle where he can row. Like Dante, Severian has two guides now: Dorcas takes the Virgil part, replacing Agia; and Hildegrin speaks for the centaur Nessus. In pointing out the sights, Hildegrin shows them the Cave of the Cumaean, which harkens to the opening of Graves' *I, Claudius* and also foreshadows the fact that the next time when they meet, Hildegrin will be in the company of the Cumaean at the Stone Town.

The name of this chapter is "Hildegrin." That the previous chapter would be called "Dorcas" makes obvious sense, but Hildegrin seems like such a minor character. Except that when Hildegrin attacks the newly raised Apu-Punchau in the Stone Town he reveals himself to be the "anti-Apu-Punchau," and thus the "anti-Severian." So, to return to the Dante track, Hildegrin really is the centaur Nessus to Severian's Heracles — he just hasn't made his assassination attempt yet.

So on the "Eschatology and Genesis" track, Severian is Adam, Dorcas is Eve, Agia is Lilith, and Hildegrin is the Demiurge.

Hildegrin gives reasons for the name of the lake: "Because so many's found dead in the water, is what some say . . . There's a great deal said against Death . . . But she's a good friend to birds, Death is. Wherever there's dead men and quiet, you'll find a good many birds, that's been my experience."

•

Our last chapter at the Lake of Birds is titled "The Flower of Dissolution," which suggests the lotus of Buddha and the illusion of reality called the Veil of Maya. Yet the first sentence has Dorcas drawing a hyacinth from the lake as if by magic, causing Severian to wonder "Is it possible the flower came into being only because Dorcas reached for it?" That the flower "materializes" stands in stark opposition to the "dissolution" of the chapter title.

In true Proustian style, the observation of this simple act (a young woman plucking a flower from the water) sets off in Severian a meditation on opposites, the nature of light and darkness, and the illusion of reality. Such thoughts add to the Buddhistic mood.

Hildegrin interprets Severian's detachment as a contemplation of his own death. Dorcas seems to think so too, and tries to talk him out of dying. It would appear that Dorcas plucked the plant of life from the water, whereas the avern Severian must get is unmistakable the plant of death.

On the King Arthur track, where would we be now? Crossing the misty waters, heading for the farther shore of Avalon — this is the "Death of Arthur" scene, the dissolution of Logres. With Dorcas as the Lady of the Lake, Hildegrin as Morgan le Fay, and Agia as the Lady of Avalon.

When Severian actually picks his avern we see not only Gilgamesh picking the Gray-Grow-Young plant (a key of eternal youth) at the climax of his otherworld quest, but also Aeneas plucking the Golden Bough of Proserpina (a key to the underworld) at the beginning of his otherworld quest, as well as the famous rites at the Lake of Nemi, where every aspirant to the priesthood had to break a certain branch as challenge and kill the priest of the sacred grove.

The avern plant looks something like a cross between an artichoke and a white rose. White roses in the Sand Garden (next door to the Garden of Endless Sleep) are linked to the white roses on the beach at the end of *Citadel of the Autarch,* which in turn are linked to the artifact known as the Claw of the Conciliator, which restores the dead to life, but the leaves of the avern are poisoned deadly daggers. Life and death, paired again. Scattered at the base of the avern are the bones of birds, alluding no doubt to the "no birds" sense of Avernus.

Shortly after getting his flower, Severian leaves the Lake of Birds in the Garden of Endless Sleep and returns to Nessus.

Looking back over these three chapters, we can see both the intricate layering and the hologrammic nature of *TBNS*. In many respects, Severian's adventure at the Lake of Birds parallels various literary and mythological underworld adventures in the afterlife. We glimpse Aeneas with his golden bough; Gilgamesh with his eternal youth plant; Dante touring hell; Heracles and Nessus; King Arthur receiving Excalibur from the Lady of the Lake, and perhaps being borne off to Avalon. Severian's experience here also prefigures his larger journey to the "real" heaven and hell of the hyperspace worldplanet Yesod, where the white flower becomes the big blossom at the birth of a new universe.

Life and death. Graveyard and garden. A vibrant new work created from the fossilized remains of World Literature.

POSTHISTORY 101

Gene Wolfe's Urth Cycle (composed of the four-volume Book of the New Sun, the novel *The Urth of the New Sun,* the novella *Empires of Foliage and Flower,* and the short-stories "The Cat," "The Map," "The Boy Who Hooked the Sun," and "The Old Woman Whose Rolling Pin Is the Sun") takes place in a future so far removed from the present as to be deemed by Wolfe himself a posthistory, balancing against the eons of unfathomable prehistory. There is a strong tradition of future histories in SF: in *The Time Machine* (1895), Wells explores the world of A.D. 802,701 and beyond, to a landscape lit by a dying red sun; and Stapledon's *Last and First Men* (1930) gives a mind-boggling view of eighteen species of man evolving and devolving across two billion years, all of which is only a footnote to his later, galactic-scale *Star Maker* (1937). There is also a tradition of science fantasists, a hybrid of science fiction realism with the trappings of quasi-medieval fantasy. The Zothique stories of Clark Ashton Smith, published between 1932 and 1948, pick up the thread of stellar death established by Wells and Stapledon with a new twist of the "future past" where mankind lives on a southern continent and dabbles with necromancy while the red sun grows cold. This notion is further honed by Jack Vance's *The Dying Earth* (1950), where the forgotten magic and superscience (nearly indistinguishable from each other) are sought after by sardonic and cunning magicians and rogues. Wolfe seems to have applied Clarke's Law to Vance's world, insisting that superscience is magic, and vice versa, and while Wolfe has openly acknowledged Smith and Vance as providing the impetus for the Urth Cycle, there is also a certain amount of Wells and Stapledon present as well. Though Wells provides dates for his future history and Stapledon gives charts of ever-increasing scale, Wolfe is much more subtle in his approach.

There are a lot of terms relating to large time scales and historical periods floating around in the Urth Cycle, and some are rather flexible. For example, the term "saros" (the Babylonian name for the number 3600, or a period of 3600 years; adopted by modern astronomers as the name of the cycle of eighteen years and ten and two-thirds days, in which solar and lunar eclipses repeat themselves) is used in both its ancient sense, by Severian ("The decades of a saros would not be long enough for me to write" [I.ii.12]) and its modern sense, by an unlettered old woman near the Stone Town: "'once or twice in each saros one of those he [Apu-Punchau] has called to him will sup with us. . . . You will recall the silent man. . . . You were only a child, but you will remember him, I think. He was the last until now'" (III.vii.51). The appendix article "Money, Measures, and Time" gives definitions for a few of these terms: "a *chiliad* designates a period of 1,000 years. An *age* is the interval between the exhaustion of some mineral or other resource in its naturally occurring form (for example, sulphur) and the next" (II, app.). All well and good, but what on Urth is a "manvantara"? What is the relationship between the various named ages (Monarch, Autarch, Myth, Ushas) mentioned in the Cycle? And what do these ages have in common with the definition given?

Severian uses the term "manvantara" for the lifecycle of a universe from Big Bang (or "Big Bloom," as he describes it [IV.xxxiv.241]) to the "Grand Gnab" (*Otter* 69) — the final collapse of matter into itself. This is appropriate, since a manvantara is a measure of time in Hindu cosmology, composed of four "yuga" or ages of the world. These four yuga correspond to the Classical Ages of Man (Gold, Silver, Copper, and Iron), which in turn brings us back to Wolfe's oblique definition connecting ages with minerals. (The reference to "sulphur" would seem to be a red herring.) For the ancient Romans as well as the ancient Hindus, the transition from a Golden Age to an Iron Age reflects a decline from a highly spiritual Edenic state to one of gross brutality. In the first age, the Krita-yuga, mankind possesses natural virtue, and there is no sadness, malice, or deceit; in Treta-yuga, duties are no longer spontaneous, they must be learned, and sacrifice and ceremony are invented; by Dwapara-yuga, disease, desire, and disaster have become commonplace, and the Rig Veda (the earliest of sacred Hindu texts) appears; and finally, in Kali-yuga the world enters a dark age of strife and warfare, where love and sex are separated, few know truth, material possessions confer rank, and outer trappings are confused with inner religion.

Posthistory, or the history of Urth, seems to be divided into four phases: the Age of Myth, the Age of the Monarch, the Age of the Autarch, and the Age of Ushas. Furthermore, there is a marked similarity between the four Hindu yuga and the four ages of Urth.

Start with the foreground and the Age of the Autarch. The majority of the action in the Urth Cycle takes place in the Age of the Autarch, an age named most conspicuously in Wolfe's article "Cavalry in the Age of the Autarch" (*Castle of the Otter*). This is the period of Urth in decline, ruled in name only by a leader of a continent in the southern hemisphere. Technology is so long forgotten that even its custodians are reduced to rite and ritual: the knowledge that the "towers" are actually rocket ships is so widely known that one begins to suspect that, despite all of Severian's dreams of them lifting into the sky at the utterance of a secret word, the ships really have fossilized into mere towers. Nowhere is nature left untouched: all the mountains have been carved into monuments to long-forgotten autarchs. Religion, too, seems to have fallen off, and as a testament to brutality, the war between the Commonwealth and Ascia, ultimately a struggle between the Other Lords and the New Sun, has been going on for at least several generations. Watching over it all, the sun itself has grown so dim that stars can be seen during the day. This is the Kali-yuga, the Iron Age.

Assembling the various hints and clues, one comes up with the following fragmentary history:

- The age begins with the first autarch, Ymar the Almost Just. Ymar is an apprentice of the jailers (the prototype of the torturers) in the last days of Typhon, but nothing is known about his rise to power. He reforms the jailers into two guilds (witches and torturers), has Father Inire build the Second House within the walls of the House Absolute, and takes the test of the hierodules by going to Yesod. He dies circa 1000 PS (Pre-Severian's reign).

- Sometime between 1000 PS to 700 PS, the Yellow Empire and the Green Empire end their war against each other, possibly in that region of the northern hemisphere later known as Ascia, with the takeover of the Green capital by soldiers in silver armor who fly a silver flag, a strong suggestion that the Mirror-people of ancient Chinese legend have come again.[1] This period probably marks the introduction to Urth of the great monsters (Abaia, Erebus, et al.), the exultant clans, and the technology of the magic mirrors. (The dates are guesswork, based on textual details suggesting

---

1. See "Fauna of Mirrors" in Borges, *The Book of Imaginary Beings*.

that the war lasts either a thousand years [*Empires of Foliage and Flower*] or a hundred generations [II.xxxi.265], that its end comes after the era of Typhon [a soldier in *Empires* says, "'By the Book! . . . What in the name of awful Abaia'" (*CRANK!* 2:27)] but before the brown book is published [as *Empires* is a story in the same].)

- *The Book of Wonders of Urth and Sky* (also known as the brown book) is a standard work from 400 to 300 PS.
- In 300 PS, Autarch Sulpicius sets aside a collection of books in the Library at Nessus. The torturers entertain a guest at Holy Katharine's feast, an event that becomes a part of guild lore (I.xi.89).
- Sometime around 210 PS (i.e., at least seven generations before Severian), the spaceship *Fortunate Cloud* crashes on Urth. Jonas is damaged in the crash, which perhaps occurred near the House Absolute, since the crew is imprisoned in the antechamber, a place reserved for people accused of committing crimes on the grounds of the House Absolute.
- In 100 PS, the witches complain about the presence of the post (used for torture) in the Old Yard of the Citadel, so it is moved into the Matachin Tower (I.xii.99).
- Circa 70 PS, Autarch Maruthas closes the roads to unauthorized traffic, giving the uhlans (a kind of highway patrol) the right to kill and loot offenders (I.xii.102). (This figure assumes that Master Palaemon is ninety years old in 1 PS.)
- A scandal involving servant Lomer (twenty-eight years old) and Chatelaine Sancha (fourteen years old) sends Lomer into the antechamber during the reign of Appian in 66 PS (II.xv.113). Odilo I serves in the House Absolute.
- In 62 PS, Chatelaine Sancha leaves the House Absolute for fifty years (*Endangered Species* 215). I assume her to be eighteen years old.

- Paeon the honey steward dies in 50 PS.
- In 42 PS, Dorcas dies in childbirth at age sixteen (I.xxxvii.176: husband searching for forty years, began the year after she died). (I.xxvi.205: she looks sixteen years old). (IV.xxxvii.264: she died in childbirth). (IV.xxxii.225: she had died forty or more years ago).
- In 31 PS, Journeyman Palaemon is exiled from the torturers' guild over a mysterious scandal (IV.xii.89), and at the same time something happens regarding the Phoenix Throne: either the "Old Autarch" (a nameless figure) begins reign, or Appian changes his ways, perhaps returning unmanned from his own trip to Yesod (II.xxiv.188).
- Around 20 PS Thecla is born; Catherine is in the Matachin Tower, and Severian is born; and the Old Autarch becomes a criminal, presumably by opening the Echopraxia brothel.
- Around 19 PS, a silent man with a staff visits the Stone Town (III.vii.51). Or might it have been as far back as 30 PS, when it could be Palaemon on his way north?
- Odilo II begins work at the House Absolute in the year 15 PS.
- In 12 PS, Chatelaine Sancha returns to the House Absolute (*Endangered Species* 215).
- In 10 PS, Thecla (assume around ten years old) sees Sancha alive (II.xv.112).
- In 6 PS, Sancha dies at age seventy-five, "a series of incidents that culminated . . . ten years ago" (*Endangered Species* 211) written by Odilo II in 5 SR (Severian's Reign).
- In 2 PS: Severian saves Vodalus' life (autumn); Thecla is sent to the torturers (winter); Severian finds Triskele and meets Valeria; Drotte and Roche are elevated to journeymen; and Severian is taken to Echopraxia (spring).
- In 1 PS, Severian has eight months as captain of apprentices, then he is elevated (winter) and eleven

days later exiled to Thrax (spring), but later he flees further north, finishing the year at the Last House (summer). Jader's sister (in Thrax) is around ten years old; and (by the above calculations relating to Sancha) Lomer is ninety-four years old.

- In 1 SR, Severian fights at the Third Battle of Orythia, becomes autarch, and marries Valeria.
- At some point early in his reign, Severian lives for a year among the Ascians (V. li.364), perhaps as a slave (*Thrust* no. 19:9).
- Odilo II tells tale of "The Cat" on Hallowmass Eve (in the full of the Spading Moon) of 5 SR (*Endangered Species* 210).
- In 8 SR, Eata is convicted of smuggling and sentenced to work as a sweepsman, but he escapes into Xanthic Lands (V.xlvi.327).
- In 10 SR, Severian embarks on his journey to Yesod, rewrites his autobiography; Eata returns to Commonwealth, has adventure of "The Map."
- Dux Caesidus, Valeria's second husband, dies in 49 SR (V.xlvi.329); an assassin dies within the Second House (V.xli.291).
- Severian returns from his trip to Yesod in 50 SR. This figure is deduced from the fact that Jader's sister is sixty or more years old (V.xliii.302) and Odilo III is serving in the House Absolute (V.xliv.313). Thus, Valeria is around seventy years old.

So an unbroken chain of autarchs link Ymar and Severian across the thousand-year gap that separates them. But what came before?

Step back a few chiliads to the Age of the Monarch. Although the House Absolute was originally built by the monarchs, most of the other details about this age are buried in legends and stories. Cyriaca's tale of the lost archives, told in *Sword of the Lictor,* contains much about the Age of the Monarch. To paraphrase: the age begins when a starfaring people (probably Asiatic, if not Chinese) leave their "wild half" (emotions, fears, and feelings) behind and establish the First Empire upon Order alone. As the Empire expands to encompass one thousand stars, the wild half is sold to the "thinking engines" (computers) and "androids" (mechanical men), who then set out to ruin their makers. They do this by releasing artifacts and building whimsical cities (recall the league-high cliff Severian works his way down in *Sword*, and reconsider the "mountain" that had sunken as a long-forgotten supercity of this age) over "a thousand lifetimes" (seventy chiliads?), and eventually this return of the wild half destroys the empire. (These fantastic cities also bring to mind the incredible supercities built and abandoned by various races in Stapledon's work.)

As well as reintroducing thoughts of fortune, revenge, the invisible world, and the like, the machines also gave each man and woman a companion (i.e., an "eidolon" or "aquastor"), unseen by other eyes, as an adviser. But the machines grow weaker over time and become unable to maintain the aquastors or build any more cities — attaining that point of senility at which they had hoped that mankind would turn against them and destroy them. But when no such thing happens, the machines call the humans that loved them the most, teach them all the things that their race had put away, and then they die. Because the machines had each tutored only one human, the humans they had taught cannot agree on a thing among themselves, and eventually each becomes a sort of hermit scribe and writes out all that he or she had learned.

After a long time, a monarch (most likely Typhon) with dreams of a Second Empire gathers up all the writings in newly built Nessus in order to destroy them. But he decides to shelter the books in case his Second Empire should fail, so the Library of Nessus is established.

The Age of the Monarch is the pinnacle of magical superscience: the source of fliers, thinking machines capable of reading minds and projecting aquastors, ships that sail between the stars, android sailors to tend them, and the rest. Adding to this legendary base, we have in *The Book* and *Urth* a glimpse of life in the era of Typhon, at the end of the age. The mountains of Urth are in their natural, un-carved state, and technology, while considered a ghost of the earlier marvels (Hadelin says of a flier, "'You don't see many anymore, sieur. . . . Most won't fly now'" [V.xxxii.227]), is still ahead of the Age of the Autarch with oxenless wains, powered riverboats, and armored giants that can carve mountains with their iron hands. Nessus is founded by Typhon, who, as the monarch of many worlds, makes his capital on Urth, the most ancient one, but later admits to Severian, "'That was an error, because I lingered too long when disaster came. By the time I would have escaped, escape was no longer open to me — those to whom I had given control of such ships as could reach the stars had fled in them, and I was besieged on this mountain'" (III.xxvi.195). The disaster Typhon refers to is the abrupt beginning of the sun's decline, and the departure of all flight-worthy starships from Urth reinforces the idea that the towers of Nessus (referred to as "hulks at the old port" in *Urth*) are only towers by the Age of the Autarch. (This is also presumably the point of departure from which Wolfe's "Long Sun" series about a generational starship has begun.) This is Dwapara-yuga, the Age of Copper. The appearance of Canog's *Book of the New Sun* (not Severian's autobiography, but the original book of this title, considered long lost by Severian's day) in this age parallels the appearance of the Rig Veda in Dwapara-yuga.

The Age of the Monarch is the great period of interstellar travel, the point of origin for those who sail between the stars, so what better place to examine two of them more closely.

The Sailor Who Stole Fire from Heaven. Hethor is a

mysterious figure, a sailor who has a secret name. As Agia says, "'His name isn't really Hethor, by the way. He says it's a much older one, that hardly anyone has heard of now'" (III.xvi.108). Severian himself notes that Hethor disappears whenever Jonas is present, and he wonders if they served on the same ship together, or if Jonas would somehow recognize Hethor (III.xvi.107). The text seems to deny that they served together, giving the names of *Quasar* and *Fortunate Cloud* for their respective ships, but then again, noting the antiquity of both characters (both are from the Age of the Monarch, from the period of the First Empire), it may be that "quasar" and "fortunate cloud" are cognates of the same ancient (and probably Chinese[2]) word, especially in light of the fact that a quasar is a cloudlike celestial body. There is also a thread of associations linking Hethor to stars: Hethor's eyes are seen as stars in Severian's night on the mountain ("his eyes . . . blazed into mine . . . I saw that the points of light I had taken for their pupils were in fact two stars" [III.xiii.87]); and his disappearance in the presence of Jonas is echoed by Severian's explanation of the star motif ("'The old legends . . . are full of magic beings who vanish slowly and reappear in the same way. No doubt those stories are based on the look of stars then'" [III.xviii.131]).

My theory is that Hethor is Kim Lee Soong, which is the most ancient name in the Urth Cycle (with the possible exceptions of Robert, Marie, and Isangoma within the Botanic Gardens). It is clear that Jonas was on a ship that crash-landed on Urth around 210 PS, that most of the crew has been subsequently imprisoned in the antechamber for seven or more generations, and that the name Kim Lee Soong causes Jonas a great deal of anxiety.

---

2. Hints that the first language of both sailors is Chinese: "(Jonas) began talking to himself in a nasal, monosyllabic language I did not understand" (III.16.120), and "(Hethor) spoke a gobbling singsong" (I.xxxv.266).

As he explains, "'Kim Lee Soong would have been a very common kind of name when I was [. . .] a boy. A common name in places now sunk beneath the sea'" (II.xv.117). Hethor, or Kim Lee Soong, was probably the captain of that ill-fated ship. I suspect that, like Prometheus, he stole his magic mirrors from Yesod (the only other person with any access to mirror technology is Father Inire, a hierodule), and, like Captain Ahab, he destroyed his ship in pursuit of his personal goals in the Briatic universe of Urth. In the following passages, Hethor's lament for a lost love suggests a death and burial in space, but on closer inspection (after reading *Urth)* it is unmistakably about Tzadkiel: "'Where has she gone? My lady, the mate of my soul? . . . Gone in her little boat. . . . She is her own ship, she is the figurehead of her own ship, and the captain . . . She has left us behind. We have left her behind'" (IV.iv.24). Hethor has clearly spent time with Tzadkiel, and this is the probable source of his powers, the magic mirrors as well as his ability to enter those non-dream trances that Severian occasionally undergoes via the corridors of Time (where the passage above takes place). Furthermore, it is possible that, as a spurned lover, a sailor fallen from grace, Hethor/Kim Lee Soong is responsible for the sudden and calamitous ailment of the old sun: the worm of white fire that Hethor uses to dispatch Vodalus resonates with the imagery of the caloyer's line about "the black worm that devours the sun" (II.iv.26).

But who is Kim Lee Soong? His name suggests that he is related to the Mandarin Sung, a Chinese family prominent in public affairs, especially Soong Meiling, who married Chiang Kai-shek (1927) and was secretary general of the Chinese Aeronautical Affairs Commission (1936–38). This provides a link to our own Earth, lost in the Age of Myth.

The Sailor Who Fell from the Sky. Jonas himself is enigmatic. Comparing his name to those of other known androids like Hadid, Hierro, Sidero, and Zelezo (the word "iron" in Arabic, Spanish, Greek, and Czech) compounds the idea that Jonas is a human name (i.e., the name of a saint), bestowed upon the android after his repair from the crash-landing that left him with a biological head and left arm. Soon after discovering the tragic fate of his fellow crewmembers, trapped for generations beyond counting, Jonas steps into the mirrors, making a break with the past and hoping to return fully repaired. In Yesod, he apparently becomes fully biological; then he returns to Urth and becomes a soldier while searching for Jolenta, only to die of a disease. Resurrected by Severian, he takes on the new name of Miles (meaning "soldier").

An argument can be made that Jonas is actually Sidero. To begin with the name, "Sidero" means more than just "iron" in Greek; it is also the name of a character from Greek mythology, the stepmother who treated Tyro with such cruelty that Sidero was killed in revenge by Tyro's twin sons Neleus and Pelias (who were otherwise very much like Romulus and Remus). The android Sidero is certainly malicious enough to make Severian want revenge (V.iii.17), but Sidero seems a twin to Jonas because of the mirroring events that befall them: Sidero loses its right arm and gains a biological arm and "head" (that is, Severian controls Sidero) when Severian climbs inside; and Sidero is the only one present when Severian dies, just as Severian stands alone after Jonas steps into the mirrors. Thus, Jonas is evolving from robot to cyborg to human, just as Severian is changing from human (the prototypical "first" Severian, who brought the New Sun without unusual help or hindrance), to solar hero-king (still bound, in part, to his material body) to godling (the state he is in through most of *Urth*).

A giant step back to the Age of Myth. Our own Earth is hopelessly lost in the dawn of the Age of Myth, but there are occasional glimpses, in the Botanical Garden's Jungle Section (the "Parisian" missionary Robert, his wife or sister Marie, and the airplane), for example, as well as the familiar "Astronaut on the Moon" picture hanging on a wall within the Citadel.

Apu-Punchau is a major figure of this age. He leads a group of agricultural villagers along the way to civilization, teaching them advanced techniques of architecture and ritual, and is later venerated as a god in a place known as the Stone Town. If this figure is the same Apu-Punchau (also known as Inti, the Sun god) who was worshiped by the Incan people, then perhaps the Stone Town is Cuzco, where the Inca dynasty was established in A.D. 1200.

The shortest span of time between the era of Apu-Punchau and the era of Severian is 19,500 years. This is based on the precession of the equinoxes, which completes a cycle every 26,000 years, and the observation that the spring stars of Apu-Punchau's day are the winter stars of Severian's. (The constellations advance through the cycle, so the stars have "shifted" three seasons.) Since I have provisionally dated the rise of the First Empire at 72,000 PS, this pushes Apu-Punchau back to 97,500 PS. (If we take A.D. 1200 as the Earth-date for Apu-Punchau, this puts Severian in A.D. 98,700.)

Later in this age we must find the "dawn-men" of Thea's tale about the terra-forming of Mars into Verthandi and Venus into Skuld. The forests of Lune are also probably sown at this time. This is Treta-yuga, the Silver Age. The sun burns brightly, modest cultivation brings forth an abundance of food from Nature, and technology is in its infancy. Religious feeling is strong: the god of the people lives among them and develops elaborate rituals to try and explain to them the future sickness and death of the sun.

Back to the future in the Age of Ushas. Little is known about the Age of Ushas. There are the gods Odilo, the Sleeper, Thais, and Pega, who are respectfully worshipped by seaside-dwelling villagers. The time-traveling Green Man must come from later in this age, as he says:

"I am a free man, come from your own future to explore your age. . . . The green color that puzzles your people so much is only what you call pond scum. We have altered it until it can live in our blood, and by its intervention have at last made our peace in humankind's long struggle with the sun. In us, the tiny plants live and die, and our bodies feed from them and their dead and require no other nourishment. All the famines, and all the labor of growing food, are ended." (II.iii.20)

In other words, the Green Men have achieved a harmony with Nature and a mastery of Time and in doing so have attained a Golden Age. This may sound a bit poetic, at first, but a careful examination of the Urth Cycle will disclose two quiet and powerful gods: Fauna, or Mother Nature, and Thyme, or Father Time. Fauna appears in "The Tale of the Town that Forgot Fauna" in *Urth,* and in *The Old Woman Whose Rolling Pin Is the Sun* (Cheap Street, 1991), where she has power over animals and the harvest. To kill an animal or pick a plant for food is to trespass on her domain, but to be nourished by internal algae is to be independent of her. Thyme is the main character of *Empires of Foliage and Flower,* where he ages as he travels west and grows young as he travels east. Thyme is also the Grim Reaper, by his own admission, "'The Increate is father to all. I take them away from him — that is my function. And I return them again'" (*CRANK!* 2: 16). But to master Time by walking the corridors of Time is to lessen the sting of death, such that, as in Hesiod's Golden Age, it is no worse than falling asleep.

And Ushas is the Krita-yuga, the Golden Age where Man is once again naturally virtuous and lives in an Edenic Garden alongside his gods. Presumably, the four gods forge the race of Green Men from among their followers. If the Green Men are not the Hieros born again, they are at least a step closer to that goal.

The Shapers of Posthistory

Having ascertained the existence of four posthistoric ages, we can now look at the overall direction and purpose of posthistory itself by looking at those who move and shape it: the hierodules and hierogrammates; the Mirror-people, the inhabitants of Yesod.

A manvantara is the cycle of a universe from bloom to bust. The Hieros were a race of men in a manvantara previous to that of Briah (Severian's universe), and they spread out through their galaxy meeting life forms and shaping them into hierodules. The Hieros died with their universe, but the hierodules escaped by entering a higher universe, Yesod, in a world-size spaceship. The Brook Madregot flows from Yesod to Briah, just as energy flows from a higher state to a lower one. The hierodules rule the Briahtic universe, trying to shape the inhabitants into Hieros. Just as the reflection of a fish within Father Inire's magic mirrors causes a real creature to materialize, so do the hierodules, reflections of their creators, try to bring the Hieros into being.

"Yesod" and "Briah" are terms from the Kabbalah, an esoteric tradition of Jewish mysticism. Yesod, meaning "Foundation," is a Sefira, one of the ten Divine Utterances of God. The Sefiroth are usually depicted in a pattern known as the "Tree of Life," with Kether ("Crown," the first Sefira) forming the top, Yesod (the ninth Sefira) forming the trunk, and Malkuth ("Kingdom," the tenth Sefira) forming the base. In Kabbalah, Malkuth is considered the Sefira of the physical universe, so it is temptingly easy to see Severian's universe as being in the position of Malkuth, connected by the path Resh to Yesod, just as the Brook Madregot connects Severian's universe to Yesod.

Unfortunately, it is more complicated than that, because "Briah" is not a Sefiroth at all, but one of the four Created Worlds that interlock with the Sefiroth.

Furthermore, its position on the Tree of Life is in the middle branches, nowhere near the base. If this is the case, then moving from Briah (essentially the cluster of Sefiroth 4, 5, and 7) to Yesod (Sefira 9) would be in a "downward" motion, away from the godhead and toward the purely physical.

All very confusing. However, the upshot of it seems to be that Severian's universe is not our own, but one more spiritually advanced than ours, closer to the godhead. Either our universe somehow crawls up the Jacob's Ladder of Sefiroth to become Severian's universe, or the process ties back into the manvantara scheme, and each new universe is another step closer to the godhead, in which case we ourselves are the Hieros!

Having brought the reader to examining his or her own face in the magic mirror, we now end this course in Posthistory 101, a rudimentary outline of future ages, undoubtedly flawed in parts where I have guessed wrong or misplaced eras, but the richly mythical tapestry that makes up the background of the Urth Cycle should be clear, as well as the different threads of genre and mystical traditions.

Fragmentary Timeline of Posthistory

The Age of Myth
97,500 PS: Apu-Punchau

The Age of the Monarch
72,000 PS: The First Empire of 1000 Stars
? : Sinking lands form Xanthic Isles
2,000: The Fall of the First Empire
1,100: Era of Typhon and the Conciliator

The Age of the Autarch
1000 PS: Autarch Ymar dies
1000–700: Yellow and Green Empires end their war

350: *The Book of Wonders of Urth and Sky* is published

300: Autarch Sulpicius sets aside books in Library

70: Autarch Maruthas closes roads

66: Scandal in reign of Appian; Odilo I serves

62: Sancha leaves (assumed to be eighteen years old)

50: Paeon the honey steward dies

40: Dorcas dies in childbirth

30: Journeyman Palaemon exiled from guild

20: (Roughly) Thecla born, Severian born, "Old Autarch" becomes criminal, Catherine in Tower

19: Silent man visits the Stone Town?

15: Odilo II begins work

12: Sancha returns

10: Thecla (ten years old) sees Sancha alive

6: Sancha dies at age seventy-five

1 PS: Most events of The Book

1 SR: Severian becomes autarch

? : Severian lives among Ascians for a year

5: Odilo II tells tale of "The Cat"

8: Eata convicted of smuggling

10: Severian embarks on journey, Eata returns

49: Dux Caesidus dies, as does an assassin in the House Absolute

50: Severian returns

Age of Ushas

150 SR: Severian awakens the sleeping gods

Works Cited

Borges, Jorge Luis. *The Book of Imaginary Beings*. Harmondsworth, England: Penguin, 1987.

Cotterell, Arthur. *A Dictionary of World Mythology*. New York: Oxford UP, 1986.

Frazier, Robert. "The Legerdemain of the Wolfe." *Thrust* no. 19 (Winter/Spring 1983): 5-9.

Graves, Robert. *The Greek Myths*. Harmondsworth, England: Penguin, 1975.

Smith, Clark Ashton. *Zothique*. New York: Ballantine Books,

1970.

Stapledon, Olaf. *Last and First Men*. New York: Dover, 1968.

Vance, Jack. *The Dying Earth*. New York: Pocket Books, 1977.

Wells, H. G. *The Time Machine*. New York: Ballantine Books, 1985.

Wolfe, Gene. "The Boy Who Hooked the Sun." *Weird Tales* no. 290 (Spring 1988) : 21-22.

———. *The Castle of the Otter*. Book Club ed. Willimantic, CT: Ziesing Brothers, 1982.

———. *The Citadel of the Autarch*. Book club ed. New York: Simon and Schuster, 1982.

———. *The Claw of the Conciliator*. Book club ed. New York: Simon and Schuster, 1981.

———. "Empires of Foliage and Flower." *CRANK!* no. 2 (1993) : 15-39.

———. *Endangered Species*. New York: Tor Books, 1990.

———. *The Old Woman Whose Rolling Pin Is the Sun*. New Castle, VA: Cheap Street, 1991.

———. *The Shadow of the Torturer*. Book club ed. New York: Simon and Schuster, 1980.

———. *The Sword of the Lictor*. Book club ed. New York: Simon and Schuster, 1981.

———. *The Urth of the New Sun*. New York: Tor Books, 1987.

****

Afterword to "Posthistory 101"

This article explicated the timeline I had created for *Lexicon Urthus* (1994).

The section "The Sailor Who Stole Fire from Heaven" ends with a bit about the historical figure Soong Meiling. This is straight from the Lexicon first edition and was cut for the second edition. It was erroneous to link Kim Lee Soong to Soong Meiling, but it was an honest mistake.

This piece uses more Science Fiction Book Club editions. On that subject, here is a FAQ entry from the first chapbook of corrections:

Q: "Why is the lexicon keyed to the SFBC edition?"

A: As a teenager I read the paperbacks and library hardcovers. Then with a hint of how important The Book would become, I made the investment after being lured into the SFBC for *The Castle of the Otter.* I began the wordlist several years later while I was living overseas, using a mixed paperback collection of US and UK volumes. This later had to be converted . . . to SFBC. All because I didn't have enough money as a teenager. Since there are so many different editions, I finally decided that listing volume and chapter would have the most utility (another conversion). (*AE&1,* p. 4)

•

A few words on Jonas. In the section "The Sailor Who Fell From the Sky" I wrote of Jonas, "In Yesod, he apparently becomes fully biological; then he returns to Urth and becomes a soldier while searching for Jolenta, only to die of a disease. Resurrected by Severian, he takes on the new name of Miles."

While that is possible, I now think it is more likely that the ghost of Jonas is drawn into the soldier's body. I do not know if it displaces the other ghost or if the body has two. That is, bringing the ghost of Jonas into a fully biological body is fulfilling Jonas's deep wish, and it happens at that moment, not before. If Jonas had returned to Urth already repaired, I cannot see why he would become a soldier and write undeliverable letters to Jolenta. The soldier wrote letters to someone who was not Jolenta.

As I wrote in *Lexicon Urthus, Second Edition:* "there seem to be two souls in that man's body. Jonas's soul was drawn down into the body of the anonymous dead soldier when Severian used the Claw upon the corpse" ("Miles" entry).

NAMING THE STAR OF GENE
WOLFE'S *THE FIFTH HEAD OF*
CERBERUS

This is for those who persist in playing with books; those who come up with answers to impossible questions, along the lines of "What song do the Sirens sing?"

Gene Wolfe's novel *The Fifth Head of Cerberus* (1972) has a lot of puzzling little details that we use to answer mysteries and make up new ones. Most of these mysteries have to do with identity, sense of self versus sense of other, and other nebulous mazy things like that. This is what the novel is rightly famous for. But in a completely different direction, there are also many details about the twin planets (Ste. Anne and Ste. Croix) and the star they orbit, and at times it seems to me that I know exactly which star this is.

Then I lie down for a while and the mood passes.

In 5HC we learn the distance from Sol, the direction from Sol, the distance of the twin planets from their primary star, and key qualities of the primary. As part of my exercise I am going to rely heavily upon the seminal *Planets for Man* (1964) by Dole and Asimov as a good benchmark of what scientific thinking of the time was.

Distance from Sol

Dr. Marsch says, "The trip from here to Earth requires twenty years of Newtonian time; only six months subjectively for me, of course" (64). This suggests two things: that the target star is within twenty light years of Sol; and the humans onboard the ship experience a time dilation of 40:1 (where twenty years are squeezed down into a half year). A time dilation of 40:1 implies a velocity between .999 c and .9999 c, ignoring the time spent accelerating and decelerating.

A first-wave Anglophone colonist reports, "I was born [on Earth] and he put her and me to sleep the way they did and when we woke up it was twenty-one years afterward" (145). I read this as meaning that the starship drives have improved in the decades since that first ship was launched.

Because of the light speed barrier, the distance cannot be greater than twenty light years; but of course it could be much less (since a starship going "only" .5 c will cross ten light years in twenty years). Then again, the use of the term "Newtonian" implies relativistic speeds in excess of .5 c; and the ratio of 40:1 implies NAFAL (Nearly As Fast As Light). (If the ratio 40:1 is due to hibernation rather than relativistic speed, then "Newtonian" would seem to be a red herring.) So I will exclude those systems closer than sixteen light years as being too close, and our resulting field has around twenty-seven star systems.

Hypothetical Flight Profile

- The ship accelerates at 4 g for 0.25 years (Newtonian), crossing 0.125 light years, and experiencing 0.21675 years (Subjective).
- The ship glides at NAFAL velocity for 19.5 years (Newtonian), crossing 19.498 light years, and experiencing 0.0665 years (Subjective).
- The ship decelerates at 4 g for 0.25 years (Newtonian),

crossing 0.125 light years, and experiencing 0.21675 years (Subjective).
- The totals: 20 years (Newtonian), 19.748 light years traveled, 0.5 years (or 6 months) experienced.

(Note: acceleration/deceleration velocities will average 0.5 c; time dilation at 0.5 c is 0.867)

Among the systems most likely to have habitable worlds, *Planets for Man* lists six star systems between sixteen and twenty light years (ly) away (data as per Dole):

1. 70 Ophiuchi A/B 17.3 ly (two stars)
2. Eta Cassiopeiae A/B 18 ly (two stars)
3. Sigma Draconis 18.2 ly (type G9)
4. 36 Ophiuchi A/B/C 18.2 ly (three stars)
5. HR 7703 A 18.6 ly (type K2)
6. Delta Pavonis 19.2 ly (type G7)

Direction from Sol

We are told that Sol is visible from Ste. Anne/Ste. Croix as a "little yellow gem" located in the tail of "the Fighting Lizard" constellation (88, 154). This constellation could be completely made up, or it could be either constellation Lacerta ("the Lizard," located at 22h 20m 35N) or Chameleon (11h 30m 80S). For Sol to appear within these constellations, the viewpoint star would (I think) have to be located around either (10h 40m 35S) or (23h 30m 80N). Unfortunately there are no stars of the proper distance in either of those two areas.

That Sol is easily visible with the naked eye is another data point. The outer range for such a condition is 55.5 light years, where Sol would be a star of magnitude 6 (Gillet, 130); from our preferred range of 17 to 20 light years, Sol would be a star of magnitude 3 (Dole, 181), comparable to the dimmer stars of the Big Dipper.

There are many mentions of other alien constellations, but they cannot help us.

Qualities of the Primary

An Earthman's diary gives us detail about the local sun:

> Anyway it's a cool climate, so the thermometer tells me; but it does not seem cool — the whole effect is of the tropics. The sun, this incredible *pink* sun, blazes down, all light and no heat, with so little output at the blue end of the spectrum that it leaves the sky behind it nearly black. (140)

The detail about cool climate might suggest that the twin planets are in an orbit near the outer edge of the ecosphere (closer to the orbit of Mars, in our system). The sunlight/star is "pink," which might mean stellar class K or M; "so little output at the blue end" reinforces this sense of a star smaller than class G.

Planets for Man feels that class M stars are too cool for consideration; K0 and K1 (the biggest of the K series) are barely possible candidates. If we target class K stars, our list of six systems is reduced to four:

70 Ophiuchi A/B
Distance: 17.3 light years
Type: ?/K5
Mass (Sol): .9/.65
Visual Color: yellow and purple

Eta Cassiopeiae A/B
Distance: 18 light years
Type: F9/K6
Mass (Sol): .94/.58
Visual Color: orange and violet

36 Ophiuchi A/B/C
Distance: 18.2 light years
Type: K2/K1/K6
Mass (Sol): .77/.76/.63

HR 7703 A
Distance: 18.6 light years
Type: K2
Mass (Sol): .76

In an attempt to isolate possible "pinkness" I have given the visual colors of some of the stars (from astronomy field guides). I was able to find a few visually pink stars, and while none of them are within the proper distance, still their existence proves that pink stars are possible: "pale rose" Aldebaran (Taurus) K5 III; "pale red" Aludra (Eta Canis Majoris) B5 Ia; "reddish" Kochab (Beta Ursa Minoris) K4 III.

Distance from Primary

The time required for a planet to move around its primary star is a function of the planet's orbital distance. If we know the length of the local year in hours we can calculate the planet's orbit in AU (Astronomical Units). The distance is crucial, since if the distance is too short the planet will be too hot (like Venus at 0.723 AU) and if the distance is too long the planet will be too cold (like Mars at 1.524 AU). "In our own Solar system, the ecosphere extends from 0.725 AU (where the illuminance is 1.9 times that of the Earth) to 1.24 AU (where it is 0.65 times that of the Earth)" (Dole, 112).

In 5HC we learn the number of days: "There were four hundred and two trees (the number of days in Sainte Anne's year)" (188). We do not know exactly how long the local days are, but there are hints, as Earth-man Marsch writes: "It gives me an unbalanced feeling, which the too-long days and stretched nights don't help. I wake up . . . hours before dawn" (140). It seems that the days are long, but not double length, so we will guess a thirty-hour day.

402 days x 30 hours = 12,060 hours
12,060 hours/ 8,766 hours (Earth year) = 1.37577

Earth years

So if the days are thirty hours, then the years are 1.37 Earth years.

This has an effect on the text, since many episodes are related to a character's age in local years. Thus, a test against the text:

- Age of seven (when Number 5 begins his new life) equals 9.63 Earth years.
- Age of twelve (when injections begin for Number 5) equals 16.5 Earth years.
- 13 years old (age of Sandwalker and Eastwind) equals 17.88 Earth years.
- 18 years old (when Number 5 enters prison) equals 24.76 Earth years.
- 27 years old (when Number 5 is released from prison) equals 37 Earth years.
- 30 years old (when Number 5 writes his tale) equals 41 Earth years.

Calculate Orbit:

P = square root of (D^3/M)

[where P is orbit in Earth years, D is orbital distance in A.U., and M is stellar mass]

1.37577 Earth years = square root of (D^3/M)

$1.8927431 = D^3/M$

Unfortunately this gives orbits that seem to fall outside the ecospheres of stars smaller than type G. For example, an F9 (like Eta Cassiopeia A) gives 1.21 AU, and a K2 (like HR 7703 A) gives 1.13 AU.

Reverse Engineering Strategy. Let's assume that the orbit is at the outer edge of the ecosphere. Into the formula above let's plug in the mass of Sol ("1") to see what we get: the answer is 1.236 AU, which is just inside the 1.24 AU figure given by Dole. This proves that, given a star of Sol-like mass, the orbit could be "habitable."

Of course, if the star is smaller than Sol, the habitability of such an orbit falls off rapidly (because the size of the ecosphere is determined by luminosity). Thus the long orbit argues for a star of type G; contradicting the visual color data (which argues for a star of type K or M).

Different approach. If the hidden name is "Wolf," as many of the names in 5HC are, our task is much simplified, because there is a Wolf series of stars, two within our target range:

- Wolf 294—(6h 52m 33N), 19.4 light years (class M4)
- Wolf 630—(16h 53 m 8s), 20.3 light years (four stars, M4, M5)

Of the two, Wolf 294 is a better bet. As a special bonus, it is located in the constellation of Gemini ("the Twins"). Seen from Wolf 294, Sol would be in the area of Sagittarius. But it would be impossible for the habitable orbit of 402 days around this dim star unless it was actually somehow a G type star in heavy disguise.

So we are back to square one — or worse, since we have added a candidate rather than reducing them!

Final Candidates
1. 70 Ophiuchi A/B 17.3 ly (two stars)
2. Eta Cassiopeiae A/B 18 ly (two stars)
3. Sigma Draconis 18.2 ly (type G9)
4. 36 Ophiuchi A/B/C 18.2 ly (three stars)
5. HR 7703 A 18.6 ly (type K2)
6. Delta Pavonis 19.2 ly (type G7)
7. Wolf 294 19.4 ly (class dM4)

The best realistic bets are Sigma Draconis and Delta Pavonis: both are G, but so much smaller than Sol (G2) that they might begin to exhibit "K type" visual coloration. I should mention that while the details of solar output point toward a K or M type star, the "pinkness" itself can also be attributed to atmospheric elements on the worlds rather than an inherent quality of the star.

The Cloaking Effect

Then again, there is another angle to be considered. Following up on the notion that the primary is a type G star that is "in heavy disguise," some thoughts on a possible "cloaking effect."

We are told the star system had been passed over by earlier colonization efforts from Earth:

> "Sainte Croix and Sainte Anne are called planetary twins; the phrase refers to more than their rotation around a common center. Both our worlds remained unknown when planets more distant from Earth had been colonized for decades." (200)

One explanation for this "overlooked" quality is that the Shadow Children were projecting an illusion spell through their singing:

> "We have sung to hold the starcrossers back. We desired to live as we wished, unreminded of what was and is; and though they have bent the sky, we have bent their thought. Suppose I now sing them in, and they come?" (129)

The text gives hints of a possible cloaking effect, which seems to have hidden the habitable planets from view or, possibly made the star seem to be of a stellar class unlikely to have habitable planets. Then the text gives a moment of unveiling:

The last Shadow child said firmly, "Nothing is

worse than that I should die," and something that had wrapped the world was gone. It went in an instant . . . The sky was open now, with nothing at all between the birds and the sun." (130)

This sounds like the cloaking effect only hides the planet rather than changing the look of the sun from other systems. Then again, there are two planets involved, so even this commonsense approach runs into complication.

If the star is cloaked, then supposition on the distance ranging from 16 to 20 light years from Sol would remain valid. It would presumably be a type G star disguised as something else, rendering moot all guessing at mass and visual color. Thus the system is hidden in plain sight: we cannot know which of the twenty-seven systems is the right one, except that it is probably the *least* likely candidate.

Bibliography

Allen, Richard Hinckley. *Star Names: Their Lore and Meaning.* Dover Publications, Inc. New York: 1963. [visual colors of stars]

Dibon-Smith, Richard. *Starlist 2000.* John Wiley & Sons, Inc. New York: 1992. [visual colors of stars]

Dole, Stephen H. and Isaac Asimov. *Planets for Man.* Random House, Inc. New York: 1964.

Gillett, Stephen L. *World Building.* Writer's Digest Books. Cincinnati, Ohio: 1996.

LIONS AND TIGERS AND BEARS ... OF
THE NEW SUN

1. The Strange Bear Man at the Threshold

The first time I read *The Urth of the New Sun*, one scene tantalized me more than any other. I could see just enough to know that there was a great deal I could not see yet. The symbols were there, I just could not understand them. It was in chapter 14, "The End of the Universe," where, in the rigging of the starship, Severian has single combat with a mutineer who has claws:

> I paused for a moment to look at him, with some vague notion that the claws I had seen might be artificial, like the steel claws of the magicians [in *The Sword of the Lictor*] or the *lucivee* with which Agia had torn my cheek, and if artificial, they might be of some use to me.
>
> They were not. . . . The claws of an arctother had been shaped from his fingers — ugly and inno-cent, incapable of holding any other weapon. (101)

The combatant he faces is a modified human who has bear claws instead of fingers, in contrast to the metal hand weapons used by both the magicians (at the foot of Mount Typhon) and Agia (at the jungle court of Vodalus). Severian triumphs against this bear-man and soon thereafter the starship passes from their home-universe Briah into the higher-universe Yesod: thus, the bear-man was in some sense a guardian of the threshold, even though as a common mutineer he was not tagged as such.

For a succinct definition of threshold guardians, I employ J. E. Cirlot:

> Just as the powers of the Earth must be defended, so, by analogy, must all mystic, religious and spiritual wealth or power be protected against hostile forces or against possible intrusion by the unworthy. . . . From the psychological point of view, guardians symbolize the forces gathered on the threshold of transition between different stages of evolution and spiritual progress or regression. The 'guardian of the threshold' must be overcome before Man can enter into the mastery of the higher realm. (Cirlot, *A Dictionary of Symbols*, "Guardians" entry)

This definition captures much of what I saw in that first glance: while it is clear that throughout his narrative Severian is undergoing an evolution changing him from a torturer into the Conciliator (and beyond), the combat with the bear-man was a distinct threshold, beyond which lay the literally higher realm of Yesod (if we take Yesod to be a kind of hyperspace).

Identifying the threshold and the guardian was all I had initially: I did not know why the guardian in this case was a bear, or better, why it *had to be* a bear. So I began to investigate what "bear" means in the text.

2. The Atrium of Time Provides a Key
In tracking down the bears in Severian's narrative, I found

myself back at the beginning again, where I discovered an important clue.

In *The Shadow of the Torturer,* chapter 4 ("Triskele"), Severian chances upon the Atrium of Time, an enclosed garden hidden deep within the Citadel complex. Emerging from the underground maze that had led him to the place, he takes in the scene:

> Statues of beasts stood with their backs to the four walls of the court, eyes turned to watch the canted dial [of a multifaceted time piece]: hulking barylambdas; arctothers, the monarchs of bears; glyptodons; smilodons with fangs like glaives. All were dusted with snow. (43)

Severian finds a garden where four types of statues are focused on a central clock that is tipped over and broken. All these statues are of animals extinct in our time: the barylambda was a cow-sized, primitive herbivore of Paleocene North America; the arctother was the very large bear of North and South America; the glyptodon, which possessed a carapace like an armadillo, was a cow-sized herbivore of South America; and the smilodon was a saber-tooth tiger. (A "glaive" is a poleaxe with a head like the blade of a sword.)

The placement of the statues suggests an opposition between arctothers and smilodons: while we do not know the orientation of the garden, opposing sides will be North/South and East/West. I tend to think that the bear/cat sides are North and South. Because the garden is literally focused on a timepiece, there is a hint that the four types of animal statues represent the seasons. As will become clear, I think that the bear represents winter and the cat summer.

The bear/cat polarity has already been alluded to just two pages earlier when Severian describes the beast handlers of the Bear Tower. Among them, "at some point in life each brother takes a lioness or bear-sow in marriage, after which he shuns human women" (I, ch. 4, 41). The big cat and the bear seem to be sacred animals, paired and yet in opposition.

3. Many of Severian's Foes Are Bear-like

Initially it seemed as though the bear-man on the starship was the first bear-like opponent that Severian fights, but as I began to look closer, many intriguing details began to emerge: Severian faces a series of ursine opponents, nearly all of whom are killed.

The first bear is Agilus. Severian's combat with him is at the Sanguinary Fields of chapter 27, but the buildup to this begins ten chapters earlier: at the rag shop (I, ch. 17, "The Challenge"), Severian is challenged to a duel by a hipparch of the Septentrion Guard. (The challenge is given by Agia in disguise; her twin Agilus later wears the same disguise for the duel). Agilus is a bear in that he is disguised as a Septentrion Guard, where "Septentrion" is another name for the constellation of the Great Bear (it became a term for the North in general). Agilus cheats at the duel, but when the dead Severian rises up from the ground Agilus panics and kills several spectators in his attempt to flee. Ironically the magistrate orders Severian to execute Agilus for his crimes against the spectators, so while Severian kills Agilus it is a legally sanctioned execution.

The second bear is Hildegrin. Hildegrin is often referred to as "the Badger," due to his digging up of corpses, but he is introduced in the first chapter of *Shadow* as being like a bear: when Thea takes the laser pistol from Hildegrin it seems to Severian "as if a dove had momentarily commanded an arctother" (I, ch. 1, 14). So twenty-two chapters before we are given his name or his sobriquet, Hildegrin is described as being a bear. At the end of *The Claw of the Conciliator* (ch. 31), Hildegrin calls for Severian's aid as he wrestles with Apu Punchau in the revived Stone Town. As Severian enters the fray, the time-warp scene implodes (due to Severian's physical contact with Apu Punchau) and Hildegrin is never seen again.

The third bear is the alzabo. This ghoulish monster animal of Urth is based upon medieval legends concerning the hyena, and yet when the alzabo appears in *The Sword of the Lictor* it clearly has bear traits: "Its fur looked red and ragged in the firelight, and the nails of its feet, larger and coarser than a bear's, were darkly red" (III, ch. 16, 128). When Severian later sees the alzabo by daylight, he notes: "It was so large and moved so swiftly that I at first thought of it a red destrier, riderless and saddleless" (135). The alzabo has bear claws, a bear's body mass, and bear fur that is red like the color of the dying sun. Severian's combat with the alzabo is complicated by the maneuverings of Agia (who wants to kill Severian) and Casdoe (the one whom the alzabo is after), so in the end Severian pledges a truce with the monster. The next day the alzabo is killed by wildmen zoanthrops, and Severian looks upon the corpse with some compassion.

The fourth bear is Decuman, one of those sorcerers alluded to in the quote about the bear-man. Shortly after the death of the alzabo, Severian encounters the sorcerers (*The Sword of the Lictor,* ch. 20 and 21), and finds them to be unmodified human males who use steel talons as hand weapons. The sorcerers kidnap Little Severian and Severian enters a duel of magic to ransom them both, but his opponent Decuman is killed by a monster (sent by Agia's agent Hethor to track and kill Severian).

Up to this point, the bear traits have been physical (claws, fur, size) or in the name (Septentrion). But bears are famous for hibernating; for going into their caves to sleep out the winter. With that hint, perhaps you will not be as surprised as I was to recognize the fifth bear in Master Ash and his Last House in *The Citadel of the Autarch*.

Severian had taken on a mission from the Pelerines to force Ash from his hermitage (allegedly to save him from the advancing Ascian forces), but once there, Severian discovers that the house is a time portal, with different ages visible from different floors, and that Ash is a man (perhaps the last human on Urth) who is watching the final ice age ("winter") from the safety of his house ("cave"). Severian sleeps in the Last House, a detail that locks in with the hibernation theme. Severian has to use force to get Ash out of the house, and when that is accomplished, Ash fades away. The next person Severian meets reminds him that it is New Year's Day.

The final bear in *The Book of the New Sun* is an unnamed "ursine man" who sets up Severian for the horse-taming test to join the military unit (IV, ch. 19, 151). Severian does not kill this man, though it is quite possible he dies in the battle against the Ascians in chapter 21.

The prominence of these bear guardians diminishes as the narrative of *The Book of the New Sun* progresses. Agilus is the central foe of *The Shadow of the Torturer,* and his victory would keep Severian from the Gate of Nessus: in order to triumph, Severian must die and resurrect himself. Hildegrin is trying to kill the promise of the Past in the form of Apu-Punchau, yet he is a lesser opponent than Agilus in that he is not the primary obstacle in *The Claw of the Conciliator.* The threshold that the alzabo is guarding is Fatherhood, while the sorcerers guard Sacrifice at the base of Mount Typhon, yet Typhon himself is a much more imposing monster of *The Sword of the Lictor,* as is Baldanders after him. Master Ash of *The Citadel of the Autarch* is an unarmed hermit who offers little real resistance, but beyond his threshold lies the threatening Ragnarok future. The destrier-trainer guards the awful world of War, but he himself, while literally marked as "ursine," plays a slight role compared to all the other "bears."

When the bear-man appears in *The Urth of the New Sun* he is diminished to the point of being a mere mutineer who is more bear than man, but the threshold he guards has grown to be the Universe itself, and for the first time Severian knowingly kills his ursine opponent.

4. Severian's Dealings with Cats Are Compassionate

Having established this pattern regarding bears, I turned my attention to the big cats in the text, searching for a possible pattern there. The cats are more elusive, their presence often showing only through a distant roar or a recent track: Severian hears a smilodon's roar when he is with Agia in the Jungle Gardens (I, ch. 20, 179); near the war front, Severian finds fresh smilodon tracks (IV, ch. 1, 11); in the Age of Myth, Severian hears a smilodon's cough (V, ch. 44, 345).

When a smilodon shows up in an embedded story, the protagonist (who is linked to Severian) twice avoids combat with the cat. In the mountains Severian reads a story from the brown book to his newly adopted Little Severian, and in that story, "The Tale of the Boy Called Frog," there is a confrontation between a smilodon and a wolf family that has just adopted the boy called Frog (III, ch. 19, 153). Combat is avoided, however, and when the smilodon appeals to the Senate of Wolves to attempt to get the boy by legal means, combat is again avoided when another animal (a big cat) ransoms Frog with gold.

Two times in the text Severian encounters big cats face-to-face, and both times they are bound creatures: while crossing the pampas with Dorcas and the dying Jolenta, Severian frees an atrox (a type of ice age cave lion) that is tied to a tree to scare off other atroxes (II, ch. 29, 270); in Typhon's Era on Urth, Severian frees a smilodon that had been tied to a post to torment a prisoner (V, ch. 34, 276). When a wounded Severian encounters cat-people they are the women-cats of the Old Autarch, who act as nurses for him, and their hidden claws remind him of the Claw of the Conciliator (IV, ch. 24, 195).

The contrast between Severian's interactions with the "bears" and the big cats is plain: the bears are foes who must die, and the cats are foes to be avoided or friends to set free. In dealing with the bears, Severian shows severity; in dealing with the cats, he exhibits mercy and compassion.

It occurs to me that Agia may be a hidden cat. After all, I have identified her twin brother Agilus as a bear, which in the scheme I have sketched would make her a cat. In addition, Severian shows mercy in not executing her outside the Mine at Saltus (II, ch. 7), which ties into the mercy-towards-cats I have traced, and Severian first hears a smilodon roar while he is with Agia (I, ch. 20). Finally, while Agia uses an athame (poisoned witch's dagger) against Severian at the Mine (II, ch. 7) and a crooked dagger against him at the widow's house in the mountains (III, ch. 15–16), she only scores a hit on him with the aforementioned lucivee (IV, ch. 26), a type of metal "cat's claws" (the name in French means "lynx"). There is also the chapter title "The Mercy of Agia" (IV, ch. 25) wherein she rescues Severian from behind Ascian lines.

5. The Meanings of This Pattern

I think this pattern of bear and cat has applications to both ecological niches and ice age mythology.

Habitual readers of Gene Wolfe have noticed that he often marks his protagonists as wolf or wolf-like, from the obvious example in the story title "Hero As Werwolf," to the more subtle case of *The Book of the Long Sun,* where Silk's pet bird is "Oreb," a biblical name for a raven associated with a wolf (Oreb and Zeeb are a pair of Midianite leaders in Judges 7:25. Oreb means "raven," while Zeeb means "wolf"). It is well known that Severian is so marked: when Severian's adoptive son asks him for a story from the brown book, he specifies that it must have "wolfs" [sic] in it; the story, as mentioned before, has the wolves adopting a human boy, just as Severian has adopted the new orphan; Severian later remarks, as he is trying to find his way out of the underground maze of the sorcerers, that "My nose is by no means the sensitive one of the he-wolf in the tale" (III, ch. 21, 167).

In writing wolf-heroes, Gene Wolfe takes a number of different approaches, depending on the story. Generally speaking, his fiction paints hunters in an unfavorable light, in part a reaction to the hunters that kill the wolf in such stories as "Peter and the Wolf" and "Little Red Riding Hood." Another approach is the wolf as predator in an ecological system, as in his "Hero As Werwolf." There is also the beast fable, such as "The Tale of the Boy Called Frog," where beasts or beastmen are relating to each other in satire of human society, that is, with little or no basis on ecological niches. In *The Book of the New Sun* as a whole, however, Wolfe seems to be taking an ecological approach at a deep level, in the same way that perhaps the Old English epic "Beowulf" is "really" about a bear ("bee wolf") who goes into a cave to fight a fire-spitting monster (bee venom as "fiery") and finds "gold" in the form of honey.

Bears are animals of the northern forests, from the temperate zone to the arctic. Wolves are also native to these areas, and in such ecological niches the bear (a large omnivore) is just above the wolf (a carnivore), sometimes preying upon it. So in ecological terms the bear and the wolf are enemies, with the bear having an advantage in single combat.

In contrast, lions and tigers are generally found in the tropics where they occupy a niche similar to that of wolves, but they are not in competition with wolves so the big cats are not enemies of wolves. Severian's reign as autarch begins with Agia as the new Vodalus, and thus she is twinned to Severian in a way that is not big cat to bear (as it was with her brother), but big cat to wolf (two equals who will keep out of each other's sphere).

So it seems to me that in this pattern of bear, cat, and wolf, Gene Wolfe is exploring the wolf within an ecological niche, where the bear is a superior foe that threatens the wolf, rather than focusing on the wolf as a predator of creatures in the niches below itself.

In addition to this personal/ecological level there is also a powerful set of mythic symbols from the ice age period of around 30,000 years ago. In *Primitive Mythology*, Joseph Campbell writes about an ice-age burial skeleton with necklace and girdle of lion teeth and bear teeth, discovered in the Landes region of southwest France:

> The bear and lion teeth are interesting, because these two animals, in the northern bear and African lion-panther rites, respectively, are, as we have seen, equivalent in form. . . . A mythological association is thus suggested of the bear and lion with the sun, solar eye, slaying eye, and evil eye, as well as with the animal master and the shaman. This must have been for millenniums one of the dominant mythological equations underlying the magic of the paleolithic hunt. (Part 4, Section 4, p. 379)

The bear and big cats are solar symbols, and despite the different geographical habitats of the animals (and their cults), it is fascinating to see that the cults did overlap in Europe to the point where the burial site would have both bear and cat represented. This clearly has some bearing on Severian's narrative, with its central solar focus.

The bear and big cat cults come from the Magdalenian period of Cro-Magnon Man (circa 30,000 to 10,000 years ago), but the bear cult seems to be older, arising in the time of Neanderthal Man (circa 200,000 to 25,000 years ago). The Neanderthals also had the curious practice of ritualistic cannibalism in which they ate the brains of their human victims. This grisly detail is re-enacted in *The Citadel of the Autarch*, where the Old Autarch's forebrain must be eaten raw by his successor, Severian (IV, ch. 29). So Gene Wolfe is using mythic material that predates Homo Sapiens Sapiens.

But the rites for both bear and cats involved placating

the spirits of the slain animals; that is, there was no pattern of killing one and sparing the other, as I have depicted in the text. This would appear to be a departure from what is theorized, and shows Wolfe working with ice-age symbols to tell a different story.

Speculatively, I offer the following interpretation. The bear, because it hibernates, represents the inconstant sun of the north; the big cats, because the winter is mild in their climes, represent the constant sun of the tropics. With a little magical thinking one can easily change cause and effect to determine that it is the bear going into a cave that causes the sun to grow weak (rather than the coming of winter that makes a bear hibernate), so that if one could only keep the bear from the cave, the sun would not weaken. Likewise, if the bear is already in the cave, if it can be driven out then a new sun/new year will begin (as seen in the case of Master Ash).

In the setting of Urth, the bear is unequivocally linked to the Old Sun, the swollen, red, dying sun that will finally go cold and leave the world in a permanent ice age, termed "Ragnarok — The Final Winter" in the text (IV, ch. 17, title). The big cat is identified with the revived New Sun, golden, strong, and undying.

With all of this in mind let us return to the Atrium of Time:

> Statues of beasts stood with their backs to the four walls of the court, eyes turned to watch the canted dial: hulking barylambdas; arctothers, the monarchs of bears; glyptodons; smilodons with fangs like glaives. All were dusted with snow. (43)

The arctother is the waning sun of Northern Winter, the smilodon is the constant sun of the tropics. The central time piece is broken, meaning that the solar "engine" is no longer working, the axis of time is out of alignment, the cycle of seasonal change is coming to a halt. There will no longer be a waxing as the Old Sun is really dying. That all the statues are "dusted with snow" points to the Final Winter that will arrive if the New Sun does not come. Contrast this with the second time Severian visits the Atrium of Time, in the final pages of *The Book of the New Sun:*

> The snow I recalled was gone, but a chill had come into the air to say that it would soon return. A few dead leaves, which must have been carried in some updraft very high indeed, had come to rest here among the dying roses. The tilted dials still cast their crazy shadows, useless as the dead clocks beneath them [in the underground maze], though not so unmoving. The carven animals stared at them, unwinking still. (IV, ch. 38, 312)

Before, the Atrium seemed locked in time; now it seems that the machine of seasonal change has been at least partially repaired; the Ragnarok Winter is no longer a certainty.

Severian is cast as a wolf fighting a series of bears, each guarding a different threshold. Most of these bears die, but Severian only knowingly kills one (the final one) in combat.

Bear	Threshold	Killed By
Agilus	Death and Resurrection	Legal execution
Hildegrin	The Past	Apu Punchau
Alzabo	Fatherhood	Zoanthrops
Sorcerers	Sacrifice	Hethor's pet
Master Ash	The Future	Eviction
Trainer	War	n/a
Bear-Man	Yesod	Combat

The bears are linked to severity, whereas their polar

opposites the big cats are linked to mercy/compassion. Once its gem casing is shattered (III, ch. 38), the Claw of the Conciliator is revealed to be a claw indeed, a claw which, by one account, appears to be that of a cat or bird (IV, ch. 8, 63) — even though it is ultimately shown to be a rose thorn, still there is this linking of Conciliator to cat; and when Severian becomes the Conciliator, he practices healing (like the Pelerines who carried the Claw; like the women-cats who carried Severian) and mercy, with fewer outbursts of severity (the storm of Os; the killing of Prefect Prisca), thus becoming more catlike (as opposed to being just anti-bear).

Because Severian (the wolf) is becoming the Conciliator (the cat), it is fitting that each threshold guardian be a bear (the polar opposite of the cat and the superior enemy of the wolf). This bear threshold is less a station of the cross than a position on the clock: an "hour of the bear" that is repeated over and over again. But this repetition is not that of a closed circle of stasis, nor an inward spiral of regression, instead it is an expanding spiral of progressive evolution.

Starting from the resonances of one puzzling scene I have traced a hidden structure to the Urth Cycle, a series of bearish threshold guardians who recede into the background, yet continue to mark the personal growth of Severian. The inclusion of both the magicians and Agia within the initial quote for this essay seems far more than merely an allusion to the bearers of claw-like weapons, rather, it is a powerful link to the polar opposites of bear and big cat.

****

Works Cited

Campbell, Joseph. *The Masks of God: Primitive Mythology*. Viking Penguin: New York, 1976. [paperback]

Cirlot, J. E. *A Dictionary of Symbols*. Philosophical Library: New York, 1962.

Wolfe, Gene. *The Shadow of the Torturer*. Simon & Schuster: New York, 1980.

———. *The Claw of the Conciliator*. Simon & Schuster: New York, 1981.

———. *The Sword of the Lictor*. Simon & Schuster: New York, 1981.

———. *The Citadel of the Autarch*. Simon & Schuster: New York, 1983.

———. *The Urth of the New Sun*. Tor: New York, 1987.

GENE WOLFE: THE MAN AND HIS WORK

John Clute has called him "quite possibly the most important" author in the contemporary sf field. Ursula K. Le Guin has called him "our Melville." Michael Swanwick has called him the greatest living writer in the English language. Who is this mild-mannered man named Gene Wolfe, and how has he won these accolades?

Through a lot of hard work, it turns out.

Gene Wolfe came to writing after returning home from the Korean War (1954), completing his college education at University of Houston, and getting married in 1956. Looking for a way to supplement his salary as an engineer at Proctor & Gamble in Cincinnati, the twenty-six-year-old newlywed began writing stories in whatever free time he could find.

His first sale came eight years later, in 1965.

To put this into perspective, at that point he had three children (of an eventual four), with the eldest already in second grade. That's a long time in "parent years."

His first novel was published in 1970, and since then he has written twenty-three more, some of them singletons, most of them set in one of several series (*The Book of the New Sun, The Book of the Long Sun, The Book of the Short Sun, The Wizard Knight,* and the *Soldier* series). His novels have won awards: the Nebula, World Fantasy Awards, Locus Awards, and British awards, among others. Although he is primarily a novelist, Gene Wolfe has never abandoned the writing of shorter works and he has seen more than 210 of them published.

His stories cover a broad spectrum of science fiction and fantasy, ranging from highbrow literary puzzles to lowbrow tabloid realism, with several odd tangents in between. He has a knack for taking a genre staple and turning it on its head. For example, an early space adventure titled "Alien Stones" (collected in *The Island of Doctor Death and Other Stories and Other Stories*) in which the starship's empath thinks like a child and the rugged captain can solve the first-contact mystery only by thinking like an engineer, seems like a topsy-turvy version of *Star Trek.*

There's some Horror, there's some Mystery, and there's some Humor. Looking across it all, certain trends become apparent in each of four decades: the seventies, the eighties, the nineties, and the present.

The Seventies: Literary Tricks

This is a trick question, but an easy one.

— Number Five

Gene Wolfe first gained attention in the 1970s through two different series of linked stories: the three novellas of *The Fifth Head of Cerberus* and the "Island" stories. His technique was to take an initial story, shift it dramatically for a second story, and then shift it again for a third story. This literary gambit paid off handsomely: the second "Island" story, "The Death of Doctor Island," won both a Nebula and a *Locus* award.

In 1972 Wolfe left Proctor & Gamble to become editor

at *Plant Engineering*, a trade journal located in Barrington, Illinois (a job he would stay with until he became a full-time writer in 1984). That year also saw the publication of *The Fifth Head of Cerberus* (1972). Set on the distant twin-worlds of Sainte Anne and Sainte Croix, these three novellas appear to be sequels sharing a common location, timeframe, and characters. Yet below this surface the reality is shifting from story to story.

The first novella, titled "The Fifth Head of Cerberus," is the memoir of an established citizen looking back with a certain Proustian tone — it is the coming-of-age story of a young man searching for identity in a baroque world of clones, shape-shifting aliens, and hybrids. His planet, Sainte Croix, while the more developed of the twin worlds, is still something of a backwater. The general technology is nineteenth century, complete with slavery, and yet his scientist father uses profits from his brothel to conduct experiments in genetic engineering.

The second novella is "'A Story,' by John V. Marsch," written by an anthropologist from Earth who is a minor character of the first novella. The story reads like an anthropological reconstruction of the shape-shifting aliens and their world, Sainte Anne, as it existed before the humans came. It is a gripping coming-of-age story about a young man in a stone-age tribal society who visits other tribes who seem at times to be as fantastic as fairies, goblins, and trolls. There is an implied tension between the anthropology and the recreation of a lost culture so strange as to seem a total fantasy — that is, between science and fiction. How much of the story is real, and "real" to what degree? How much of the story is a projection of the anthropologist's life and/or dreams?

The third novella, enigmatically titled "V.R.T.," reveals that the "John V. Marsch" who wrote the previous story is a political prisoner held by a corrupt and authoritarian regime. He might be insane. He might not be a real anthropologist. He might not even be from Earth. The text itself is a hodgepodge of taped interrogations, snippets from his journal, scribbled notes, and the everyday distractions of the officer reviewing his case.

These novellas together form a dazzling, multifaceted whole that is much more than the sum of its parts. It was considered Wolfe's major work until the arrival of *The Book of the New Sun.*

Wolfe wrote a second linked-story series (starting before *The Fifth Head of Cerberus* yet finishing after it), this time revolving in a freewheeling style around three words: Island, Doctor, and Death. (These three stories are collected in *The Island of Doctor Death and Other Stories and Other Stories.* A fourth one appeared in the eighties, but that's another decade.)

In "The Island of Doctor Death and Other Stories" (1970), a lonely young boy lives with his mother at an isolated house on the coast, a house sometimes surrounded by water at high tide. His mother has two suitors: one a man her own age who drives a sports car, and the other an older physician. The woman is addicted to drugs, but the boy is addicted to genre fiction to a degree that might be worse: he identifies with the first suitor as a flashy, heroic character and thinks of the other man as "Doctor Death." As reality begins to break down, the story partakes of the "psychological thriller" or "magical realism" schools of fiction, depending upon reader interpretation.

Some years later came "The Death of Doctor Island" (1978), in which a psychologically disturbed teenage boy seems to be on a tropical island, but the place is actually an orbital mental institution run by a computer, and there are other patients who are, perhaps, more important. This time the boy is inside of a love triangle, rather than just observing. What follows is a tug of war between reality and illusion in the gray area between torture and treatment, through what might be high tech "magic" performed by Doctor Island or simply the boy's hallucinations.

The third story is "The Doctor of Death Island" (1978). Its hero is Alan Alvard, inventor of speaking books, who is in prison for killing his business partner to keep control of his singular invention. He works as an orderly in the prison hospital where there is an old doctor with a terminal ward at the seventh floor — Alvard thinks of this ward as Death Island, the tip of a submerged mountain that is the rest of the hospital, and has recurring nightmares about the doctor coming for him.

Two years into his sentence, Alvard develops stomach cancer, so he is put into experimental cryogenic suspension. Forty years later he is awakened and cured, only to find himself in a future where everybody has immortality and he is still serving a life sentence. He discovers that the government has stolen his patents in the interests of its own security (a different sort of "national security"), but in his secret and methodical way he devises an elaborate plan for escape that involves bringing fictitious characters of Charles Dickens to life. The love triangle is tangled, complicated, and submerged, yet still at the mysterious heart of the story. Here the mature hero is active in fighting for his escape from the "Island," but at the cost of making him less sympathetic than the boys of the previous stories.

Wolfe was known in the seventies for such highly structured literary tricks. He hasn't stopped, really, since he does that with novels, but in shorter works after the seventies he often uses art to conceal art.

The Eighties: Deepening Horror

Neal and Ted held her, and Jan put the sword through her belly — so she'd live long enough to know what was happening.

— Ming

It is a paradox that Gene Wolfe is not a Horror writer and yet his stories very often have a strong thread of horror to them. In the early 1970s this horror was kept a step removed from the reader by narrative distance which made the horror more cerebral, intellectual, or even philosophical. During the late seventies and through the eighties, Wolfe closed this gap, producing horror that is immediate, visceral, and gruesome.

"Silhouette" (1975, collected in *Endangered Species*) presents a starship in orbit around an Earth-like planet after a very long search from a ruined Earth. The captain wants to declare it ready for human colonization as soon as possible, and she is intolerant of dissenting opinion. Officer Johann has misgivings about the world, but he also seems to be in some sort of dream-like first-contact with something down on the surface, a non-corporeal being that is a shadow and uses darkness. When hints of his strange condition spread through the ship, secret cults emerge from hiding in the hope of starting a new religion. The story takes on a frightening and ambiguous demonology within the context of a *Star Trek*-like space adventure.

"When I was Ming the Merciless" (1976, collected in *Endangered Species*) is one side of a dialogue between a college student and his jailors. The contrast between the whimsical title and the opening scene is stark, and while a monologue might seem "distancing," in this example it actually destroys distance.

"Redbeard" (1984, collected in *Storeys from the Old Hotel*) is a conversational story about a local man with a bad reputation in rural Illinois. This haunting tale touches on fairy tales at points and zigs when you think it will zag.

"Lord of the Land" (1990, collected in *Starwater Strains*) gives us Dr. Sam Cooper, an "Indy Jones" of folklore, visiting rural Tennessee to investigate a local legend about an unusual monster called a "soul-sucker" that a trio of shooters hit at twilight. Dr. Cooper spends the night at his informant's old farmhouse and discovers a Faulknerian dynamic to the family, but as the night deepens he is drawn across time and place to face the sort of cosmic horror that would make Lovecraft proud.

While horror has always had a place in Wolfe's work, during this period a visceral horror burst out, expanding the range and engaging the reader in new ways.

The Nineties: Blazing Emotional Core

I'd like to eat the hippos.

— Rex

During the nineties Wolfe's short fiction developed a noir, almost hardboiled style, yet the emotional content was paradoxically more direct rather than being downplayed in tough-guy attitudes or cold intellect.

"The Ziggurat" (1995, collected in *Strange Travelers)* has a retired engineer going through an ugly divorce. Like a Hemingway hero he has been holed up in a remote cabin for several months, where his progress at taming a coyote has prevented him from committing suicide with a rifle. He feels used up and on the verge of being discarded, but when his wife arrives, expecting him to sign the divorce papers, he rises up with a new determination to refuse the divorce and save the marriage. When she tries to leave in her car she is assaulted by a bunch of boy-sized aggressors who make off with one of the children. The hero sets out to find her in the falling snow, and down by the lake he meets the fey alien creatures that have abducted her. It is solid science fiction, with elements of horror and fantasy, and traces of tabloid realism.

"Petting Zoo" (1997, collected in *Strange Travelers)* is perhaps Wolfe's most humorous story. A man stands in line at a children's zoo to get a ride on a most unnatural creature — a genetically re-engineered Tyrannosaurus Rex, with purple skin. Built by a boy, once, long ago. This story somehow expresses the manic energy of a "Calvin and Hobbes" comic strip merged with a welcome jab against

Barney the dinosaur, and has always seemed to me to be a perfect candidate for a Pixar animated short.

"The Walking Sticks" (1999, collected in *Innocents Aboard)* is tabloid-realism written in a folksy confessional style. (But art conceals art: it is really a crypto-literary story!) The working-class narrator receives a large crate sent from England to his ex-wife, whose current location is unknown. He and his new wife open the crate to find a cabinet filled with a collection of twenty-two unique canes. They are haunted, it seems, and at times they go out on their own to commit mayhem and murder.

Following the rising tide of horror in Wolfe's work during the eighties, the nineties marked an upsurge of powerful emotions from the heart as well as from the spleen.

The Millennium: Wolfe at Work

Tom flourished his stick, hearing Nero roar behind him and knowing that if even one other cat became involved it was all over.
— "On a Vacant Face a Bruise"

So far this decade, Wolfe's work continues to show its customary variety, with a renewed interest in dreams and nightmares. Earlier stories involving dreams include "Forlesen" (1974, collected in *Castle of Days)*, "To the Dark Tower Came" (1977, collected in *Storeys from the Old Hotel)*, and "The Detective of Dreams" (1980, collected in *Endangered Species)*.

"Hunter Lake" (2003, collected in *Starwater Strains)* is a dream that teeters on the verge of nightmare. The dreamer is Ettie, a woman who returns to a time and place when she was a teen living with her mother Susan. Susan wants to visit the haunted Hunter Lake so she can write a magazine article, but Ettie has premonitions (or perhaps memories) about the lake and she drags her feet. Following the logic of dreams, different eras are collapsed into a strange "present time." The story is a ghost story, a girls' mystery, a spirit quest, and a puzzler touching on mothers and daughters.

Strange Birds (2006), published by Dreamhaven, is a chapbook of two stories inspired by the haunting art of Lisa Snellings-Clark. The first story, "On a Vacant Face a Bruise," is an interstellar circus story that might be in the same universe as Urth and addresses the archetypal dream of "running away to join the circus." It shares affinities with "The Toy Theater" (1971, collected in *The Island of Doctor Death . . .)* and "No Planets Strike" (1997, collected in *Strange Travelers),* and I wonder if I'm alone in detecting a bit of Fellini's *La Strada* in there as well.

The other story, "Sob in the Silence," is the creepiest story Wolfe has written to date, and that is really saying something.

•

We are like children who look at print and see a serpent in the last letter but one, and a sword in the last.

— Severian

This, then, is Gene Wolfe — an engineer who transmuted himself into an alchemist through literary tricks in the seventies, summoned flesh-crawling horrors in the eighties, worked wild passions like an animal trainer in the nineties, and who currently distills the dreamworld for the entertainment and edification of readers everywhere.

But don't read him just because he is "good for you," read him because he is the best in the world, or, even better, because you like to.

THE DEATH OF CATHERINE THE WEAL AND OTHER STORIES (1992)

This essay was written for John Clute's proposed book of essays on Gene Wolfe's fiction. Back in the early 90s, before the Internet as we know it existed, I was posting messages on the Gene Wolfe topic at GEnie (it was a message board system). Before long, Gregory Feeley kindly suggested that I write an essay for Clute's upcoming book. It seemed at the time that the book would be published by 1994. It may well be that my essay killed the whole project with its leaden prose. I once read it aloud at a bookstore and literally put people to sleep — good people, I might add.

The publication of Lexicon Urthus *(1994) was still in the unknown future when I wrote this, but the Lexicon did exist in manuscript form and was looking for a publisher. So in many ways, the essay was intended to be an overture for the Lexicon, showing a bit of the work ahead of time.*

Now it serves to celebrate the publication of Lexicon Urthus, Second Edition *(2008). In preparing the essay, I initially thought I'd insert commentary in the Clute style, using square brackets, pointing out details where my thoughts in 2008 are different from those in 1992. But upon looking it over, warts and all, I find I'd rather not clutter it up more than it already is. Instead I will put that energy into a new Wolfe essay altogether.*

So without further ado, allow me to present the essay itself: hidden for sixteen years, a "lost overture" to lexicons past and present.

Catherine has been getting a lot of attention of late, not merely as the most-likely mother of Severian the Great, but also as the secret identity of the Old Autarch himself, according to John Clute (1986) and Gregory Feeley (1991). Clute and Feeley devised the epithet 'the Weal' for this hypothetical autarch Catherine, a term which I will borrow for my own purposes.

One cannot quarrel with the notion of Catherine as mother of Severian, and the family tree now seems fairly clear and straightforward: Dorcas and "Charonus" (if one can label anonymous characters by their role in the text) begat Ouen, Ouen and Catherine begat twins Severian and Merryn, or Severian and the mandragora (if this last is not actually the mandrake root its name suggests), or, least probable, all three. On the other hand, the notion that Catherine is the Old Autarch appears less likely, in spite of the fact that it would seem to solve a central mystery of *The Book of the New Sun:* the name of the autarch and the motive for keeping it secret.

In the middle of such a quagmire, it is good to go back and re-examine the source of the controversy. From whence springs Catherine the Weal? Largely from the combination of: 1) textual evidence pointing to a biological relationship between Severian and the Old Autarch, and 2) textual evidence that a monial named Catherine is Severian's mother. Does the evidence regarding the Old Autarch suggest he is Severian's mother? No, it suggests that the Old Autarch is Severian's father, but this is a theory shattered for most readers by the later evidence regarding Ouen, so the 'Old Autarch as mother' idea puts on an extra twist to maintain the theory of a biological link. Is it necessary that the Old Autarch be a biological parent of Severian? No, a spiritual parent would be sufficient.

That Catherine occupies a central role in *The Book of the New Sun* is attested to by the original title Wolfe gave to the work (which he supposed would be a novella): "The Feast of Saint Catherine." In *The Castle of the Otter*, he outlines the original plot:

> Severian, an apprentice torturer, meets a lovely prisoner, Thecla, and falls in love with her. He becomes a journeyman . . . but continues their relationship. Eventually, she pleads with him for the means of suicide, and he leaves a knife in her cell. When he sees blood seeping from under her cell door, he confesses what he has done.
>
> Eventually . . . he becomes a master . . . The guild has been forced to forgive him, and he has almost forgiven himself. Then he receives a letter from Thecla. The suicide was a trick, permitting her to be freed unobtrusively. Soon she will be exonerated and restored to her former position in society. She says that she still loves him, though it may be that she only feels guilty about using him as she did. She invites him to join her.
>
> What is he to do?
>
> As an honest man and a patriot — and he is both — he should denounce the whole affair; but if he does so, he will be disgraced again, the guild will be disgraced, and Thecla will almost certainly die. If he does as she asks, he will be reunited with her; but he will be a pariah . . . and he may well make her a pariah too, in which case she will probably come to hate him. If he simply burns her letter and ignores her, she will only come to hate him much sooner, and she will be in a position to exert great political influence, and to blackmail the other masters of the guild as well. (Needless to say, I had a solution — but I will leave it as an exercise for the reader.) (4)

A solution that would tie in with the proposed title would be for this Severian to kill and eat Thecla, using the analeptic alzabo to preserve and imprison his beloved within the citadel of his own flesh. She would 'live,' but only inside of him. He would take on this terrible burden to protect her, his guild, and himself. (It is also a nasty thing to do to her, which seems appropriate.) Most importantly, just as the Feast of Saint Catherine marks the elevation of torturer from apprentice to journeyman to master, so does the cannibalism of Thecla represent a further stage, wherein the figurative 'feast' becomes grotesquely real: the mystery of communion made concrete. At the moment she is consumed, Thecla becomes Catherine, rendered immortal by her killer, enshrined within a torturer's cells.

However, that story was never written, and the mystery of Catherine was driven further beneath the surface, to mingle with the other mysteries, the most prominent being the identity of the Old Autarch, and at first glance, 'Catherine the Weal' seems like a most fitting answer to the autarchial question. But the keystone of the Autarch Catherine theory would appear to be a deeply rooted prohibition against dynastic autarchies, as Clute notes: "Autarchs . . . are forbidden to found dynasties" (Clute, *Strokes,* 171). This, then, is the dark sin Severian's narrative covers up: that Catherine is autarch and her son inherits the throne. But a passage in *The Book of the New Sun* rules out this dynastic prohibition, for the Malrubius aquastor tells Severian, "If you fail, your manhood will be taken from you, so that you cannot bequeath the Phoenix Throne to your descendants" (IV, chapter 31, 214), that is to say, if he refuses the test, he *can* bequeath the throne to his offspring. An autarch can either stay on Urth and hand down the throne to his or her children, or an autarch can take the test, but the punishment for failure is desexing. Malrubius' threat makes no sense in a world where dynasties are prohibited. Given that the position of autarch is open to either gender (most of the autarchs have been 'common men and women' [IV, chap. 34, 236] and then there is the term 'autarchia') dynasties in the thousand-year Age of the Autarch have probably been the rule rather than the exception.

Perhaps this reading of the supposed prohibition is a bit too literal, i.e., it is not that all autarchs are forbidden to found dynasties, but only those who fail the test. In this case the prohibition comes from Yesod rather than the Commonwealth, and Catherine has merely hedged her bets by cheating and having a child before taking the test. *The Urth of the New Sun* seems to discredit this notion:

> "Sieur," I said, "I can remember the examination of my predecessor." . . .
>
> Tzadkiel nodded. "It was necessary that you recall it; it was for that reason he was examined."
>
> "And unmanned?" The old Autarch trembled in me . . .
>
> "Yes. Otherwise a child would have stood between you and the throne, and your Urth would have perished forever. The alternative was the death of the child. Would that have been better?" (Urth, chap. 21, 153)

The Hierogrammate Tzadkiel (whose name is that of a Kabbalistic Angel of Justice) alludes to hereditary autarchy, and also suggests that the relation between Severian and the Old Autarch is not one of child to biological parent. It seems unlikely, in a universe where Hierodule agents backtrack through the corridors of Time seeking verification, and even human high priestesses such as those of the Pelerines possess the ability to detect falsehood, that Tzadkiel has been duped.

So then why the big mystery?

To begin with the obvious, there are a few practical reasons why the Autarch is never named. As the top of the power pyramid in the Commonwealth, an autarch should be so distant from the common people as to be faceless. One need only remember Emperor Showa (Hirohito) of pre-War Japan to find a recent case where citizens were forbidden to look upon the face of their leader, in person or in picture, because to see the emperor's face is to recognize him as human, and he is not human; rather, he is at the very least the embodiment of an institution. In the Urth Cycle, this lofty distance is reflected in the very mountains themselves, each of which has been carved into the likeness of an autarch, such that they border every horizon, ubiquitous yet far removed.

Another point is that names themselves have a great deal of magic: to know a person's name is to have power over him, and fairy tales are full of cases where this alone is enough to undo a character, or slay a monster. Between text and reader, or ruler and populace, a name gives an immediate sense of mystery-dispelling familiarity, the difference between 'His Majesty, the King' and 'King Mark.' By knowing the ruler's name, a pauper becomes a peer of the realm, in a sense. A third point is that names often disclose gender, and gender mystery is one of the main attributes of the Autarch. This mystery hints at the alchemical ideal of the hermaphrodite, where opposites are united, and sets the stage for the alzabo-induced chemical hermaphroditism of Severian (at which point it is seen as an abomination) as well as the Autarch (where it is revealed to be a prerequisite of leadership). The anthropological importance of this notion is clear, as such a revelation is usually the climax of 'primitive' male initiation rites around the world, wherein the headman, for example, proves that he has a 'vagina' (subincision of his penis) which bleeds when he re-opens it, simulating menstruation and the female-power associated with it. That this institutional position of autarch be faceless, nameless, and genderless is very important to the story, as Severian must first serve it as a torturer, then rebel against it as a Vodalarius, and finally come to terms with it by becoming it. And in the end, the name is nothing, the title (and the myriad lives it contains) is everything. 'Here Comes Everyman,' indeed.

Some readers (including Feeley) have made pointed reference to the use of the term "Old Autarch" in *Urth* as an uncharacteristically clumsy attempt to maintain the mystery of the autarch's name. To this way of thinking, Severian is the one who should be called the Old Autarch, as Valeria has sat upon the throne for forty years. However, the period in question is still Severian's reign. While this might seem to be merely a technicality, Valeria does not know the words of power, and there is no doubt that even the common people know this, as Eata tells Severian: "your autarchia, she was Autarch. People talked about it . . . and they said she didn't have the words" (V, chap. 46, 328). So despite Valeria's forty years on the throne, her marriage to Dux Caesidius, her title of Autarch, and the presence of Severian's cenotaph, Valeria is still regent, Severian is still autarch, and his predecessor is still the Old Autarch.

In place of Catherine, consider the autarch Appian of "The Cat" (1983) as the autarch of *The Book of the New Sun*. He reigns during the scandal that sends Lomer into the antechamber; and since Lomer yet lives when Severian comes to the House Absolute, it is certainly possible that Appian might still rule. (See timeline.)

The informant on this tip is none other than Odilo II, the servant of the House Absolute whom Severian meets on his first visit, an insider who would be privy to all the secrets. His tale "The Cat" mentions no other autarch, yet it covers seventy-odd years of life within the House Absolute. As all of the Odilos seem to have a great love for the pomp and glory of the House Absolute, it would seem strange and out of character for him to neglect mentioning the ascent of a new autarch. Catherine the Weal, had she been autarch, would have to have gone to

Yesod and been desexed sometime after the birth of Severian (roughly 20 years PS, or Prior to Severian's reign) and before Thecla comes to the House Absolute (around 9 PS), since Thecla knows the Old Autarch, but again, Odilo II mentions nothing of the kind in recounting his early years as servant (beginning 16 PS).

It has been established that the Old Autarch spent his childhood in Famulorum village (Latin 'famulor': to be a servant), near the House Absolute (V, chap. 40, 284), that he served under the honey steward Paeon, and that he gained the throne by chance rather than design. (I use the male pronoun under the assumption that domestic service jobs are usually gender segregated, at least for novice and supervisor. Another small doubt against Catherine.) One likely motive for his anonymity is that his name harkens back to his humble origins, thus servants and residents alike would look askance at him, remembering him as a lowly servant. As the Autarch says, "I was a servant once . . . That is why they hate me." (IV, chap. 25, 176)

As *Urth* makes clear, the Old Autarch's function, both in the story and in the world, is to prepare the way for Severian. His career and his trial mark the road the New Sun must follow. So Appian is a fittingly evocative name for him. 'Appian' is close to the Latin 'apia' (bee), an apt name for a servant under the honey steward, but it is closer to the Appian Way, the oldest and best preserved of all Roman roads, commenced by Appius Claudius, the censor, during the Roman Republic. There are also two saints Appian, and all three of these Appians can be said to have paved the way for others to follow.

There are a few weak points to the candidacy of Appian. While there is no doubt that there is an Autarch Appian, the question is the length of his reign: he is either 'Appian the Lesser,' reigning from 66 to 31 PS, succeeded by an as yet unnamed autarch; or he is 'Appian the Elder,' reigning from 66 to 1 PS. A sixty-five year reign might seem impossibly long (despite Hirohito's reign of 64 years) but for the apparent natural longevity on Urth (Odilo I serves for more than 50 years, and even lifelong prisoner Lomer is 95 years old), possibly augmented by stellar-level technology available to the autarch, and the time distortions caused by riding a ship to Yesod. In addition, a long reign makes it more reasonable to think that, by the time of Severian, his name might have been hidden or forgotten, such that nobody in the country could know it but the senior (and needless to say, discreet) servants.

The crisis point in 30 PS, the point at which Appian is decided to be Elder or Lesser, is alluded to in Dr. Talos' play, *Eschatology and Genesis:*

Prophet: "I know you for a practical man, concerned with the affairs of this universe alone, who seldom looks higher than the stars."

   Autarch: "For thirty years I have prided myself on that." (II, chap 24, 202)

The theatrical autarch, based in part upon Dr. Talos' surprising knowledge of the reigning autarch, seems to indicate that he has ruled for thirty years — or that he has been a changed man, a man unconcerned with Yesod, for the same period. The latter suggests the time of the desexing. Another curious little mystery in or around 30 PS is the exile of Journeyman Palaemon, and it is intriguing to consider how this scandal could be related to the autarch's failure in Yesod, or to the original idea for "The Feast of Saint Catherine."

Palaemon is an odd duck: his name is both that of a saint and that of a classical god. This is an important signal, because throughout the Urth Cycle, followers of the New Sun are named after saints, while Enemies of the New Sun (Abaia, Erebus, Typhon) are named after mythological figures. Saint Palaemon is rather nondescript, but Palaemon the god bears some looking into: he was originally the mortal Melicertes, and became the marine god Palaemon when his mother Ino cast herself with him into the sea. Ino became Leucothea, the White Goddess who figures so prominently in Wolfe's *Soldier* novels and *There Are Doors*. In any event, like Appian's way to Yesod, Journeyman Palaemon paves a way for Journeyman Severian, a precedent for having him exiled rather than executed.

As solid as the evidence may be, Appian the Elder in no way addresses the particular elusive mystery of why the Autarch's name is never written in Severian's narrative, as Catherine the Weal at least attempts to do by answering "what is being hidden?" with "Severian's mother is autarch." Rather than assailing that vast and nebulous region, this paper will now endeavor to speculate upon a few minor mysteries, in the pioneer spirit of both Clute and Feeley, in an attempt to ascertain the hidden identities of Catherine, Thecla, and Juturna.

Catherine the teenage Pelerine

To begin with, let us assume that Catherine was born an exultant (if there is an exultant in Severian's family tree, this appears to be the most likely spot), perhaps of the same family as Thecla and Thea. The historical Saint Catherine was also said to have been an aristocrat.

At a young age she joins the aristocratic Pelerines ('professional virgins' who accept primarily exultants), and travels with them, much as Cyriaca did (III, chap. 5, 37).

At the age of thirteen or fourteen she meets Ouen in Nessus, probably through the by-then defunct cloisonné shop that had sold crucifixes to the Pelerines (as Feeley proposes). Dorcas' side of the family had made the crucifixes, and they doubtlessly had connections to the Order. Ouen's mother Cas (a.k.a. Dorcas) had apparently died giving birth to him, but when her husband dropped her into the Lake of Endless Sleep, her eyes opened, an event both of them remember. This suggests that Dorcas was a victim of foul play on the part of the Enemies of the New Sun, who saw that her grandson would become vitally important and tried to interfere by putting Dorcas into a deathlike trance. So Dorcas died by drowning, and her husband was an unwitting murderer. The event made a Charon out of him and gave her an intense fear of water.

Catherine either leaves the Order for some unknown reason (as Clute and Feeley suggest), or she becomes pregnant by Ouen and then leaves under threat of expulsion. We are reminded throughout the Urth Cycle that an exultant teenage girl has the stature of a woman: Severian's fever dream of Thecla at his height (around 6'1") when she was thirteen or fourteen (IV, chap. 4, 24), and the scandal involving Chatelaine Sancha (14 years old) and Lomer (28 years old) provides a parallel for what might have gone on between Catherine (13 years old) and Ouen (20 years old).

She is taken into custody in order to protect the unborn Severian from the Enemies of the New Sun (who had so nearly gotten Ouen), rather than for any criminal activity on her part. She gives birth in the Matachin Tower, one of the most heavily guarded and secure places on the planet, which also happens to have easy, permanent access to the Atrium of Time. (The Atrium is as much a time traveling building as the Last House is.) The mother of the guild becomes the mother of the man.

After giving birth, Catherine lives in the Atrium of Time complex, coming out once every subjective 'year' for the feast day. This is why she is never seen on any other day, and why she never changes: she never ages, and while tall for a commoner she is perhaps below average height for an exultant teenager (in fact, she might be a khaibit). Valeria, Severian's future bride, is unquestionably living in the Atrium complex, safe from enemies. Severian says of Valeria, "There was an antique quality about her . . . that made her seem older than Master Palaemon, a dweller in forgotten yesterdays," and then that her family "had waited, at first, to leave Urth with the autarch of their era" (I, chap. 4, 34). Valeria's family is likely to have entered the complex around the time of Ymar's successor, a thousand years earlier.

Finally, when the deluge transforms Urth into Ushas, it is quite possible that Catherine takes to the corridors of Time, becoming the Holy Katharine tortured by Autarch Maxentius early on in the Age of the Autarch. She becomes her own sainted namesake, just as her son Severian goes through various 'incarnations' as Apu-Punchau, Conciliator, Autarch, and New Sun. The mother of the man becomes the mother of the guild.

While Catherine is the most elusive of all the women in Severian's life, her namesake St. Catherine is one of the most popular saints of all time, despite the fact that she probably never existed. Like Palaemon, Catherine is a figure with Christian as well as pagan roots. Catherine of Alexandria is said to have been a maiden martyred in A.D. 310 under Maximus Daza, and legend has it that she argued with fifty pagan philosophers before she was to be put to death by means of an engine fitted with a spiked wheel. (She overcame them all, and on this account she is considered the patroness of philosophers.) Then the wheel broke (legend adds roses bursting forth) and she was beheaded instead. Her alleged relics have been enshrined for the last thousand years in the Orthodox monastery of Mt. Sinai, but in 1969 her name was dropped from the liturgical calendar.

For the pre-Christian Catherine, a closer examination of the rosy/fiery Catherine Wheel is in order. Roses and fire are iconically nearly identical (a fact that Wolfe is well aware of: note how Frog calls fire 'red flower' [III, chap. 19, 136], and at the original center of Catherine's cult in Sinai, the Asiatic Goddess was once depicted as the Dancer on the Fiery Wheel at the hub of the Universe. In the 8th century A.D., a Greek convent of priestess-nuns at Sinai called themselves *kathari,* meaning 'pure ones,' but this name is also akin to the kathakali temple-dancers of India, who performed the Dance of Time in honor of Kali, Goddess of the Karmic Wheel. A group of medieval Gnostics known as Cathari had great reverence for the wheel symbol, and considered St. Catherine almost as a female counterpart of God. Catholic prelates made efforts to have St. Catherine eliminated from the canon in the 15th and 16th centuries, after the Cathari were exterminated. So if Saint Catherine has a hidden name, it might well be 'Kali.'

Thecla the nocturnal huntress

Allusions have been made to the correspondence between Thecla and St. Thecla, but no note has been made of the fact that St. Thecla is one of the most spurious saints in the canon. The legend of St. Thecla comes from an apocryphal document, the *Acts of Paul* (c. A.D. 170). It says that she was converted to Christ by St. Paul. She broke off an engagement to marry and dedicated her maidenhood to God, whereupon she was subjected to much persecution, in the form of attempts to kill her by fire and wild beasts. She retired to a cave where she lived for many years (recall the mine at Saltus). At the age of ninety she was again persecuted, by local medicine men who were jealous of her healing powers; she was saved from their hands by being swallowed by her cave, ending her martyrdom.

'Thecla' (meaning 'famous one') was a title of the Maiden Moon Goddess Artemis at Ephesus (now western Turkey), where she was worshipped in her second aspect as Nymph, an orgiastic Aphrodite with a male consort. Her shrine in Seleucia (Mesopotamia) was a popular pilgrimage center in pagan times, and remained so even after the goddess was Christianized as a saint. Tertullian (3rd century Roman theologian) knew she was nothing but an epithet of the Great Goddess, and he denied the legend connecting Thecla with St. Paul, hinting that Paul might have been honored by the connection. So Thecla's hidden name might be 'Artemis,' and with this in mind, the unbelievable trials of St. Thecla can be recognized as the same sort of goddess rites that Inanna, to give an early example, had to perform.

So in Wolfe's Thecla, with her memories of hunting both beasts and humans (the attacks on the prisoners in the antechamber), we find another disguised goddess.

Juturna of the deep

A third mother figure for Severian is the undine Juturna, and hers is the name of a Roman water-goddess, responsible for putting out fires. Her name gives no pretense at being anything but an Enemy of the New Sun (a mythological name and a water-related one as well), and as concubine to Abaia, Juturna's motives for sporadically helping Severian are obscure: she gives rebirth to him at the beginning of *The Book of the New Sun*, but later tries to lure him into drowning. She seems unique among her kind in being able to travel the corridors of Time, and she survives the deluge: these two points may form her motive (i.e., she has seen the future and is picking the winner). Aside from a cameo in a corridors of Time episode (IV, chap. 4, 25), Juturna appears four times in the Urth Cycle:

1) rebirth of Severian in volume one,
2) attempted drowning in volume two,
3) her warning of deluge in *Urth,* and
4) pointing out the way to Brook Madregot in *Urth.*

From her point of view as a time traveler, the order should probably be rearranged as 2-3-1-4.

Juturna is important for showing the link between what might be too readily termed 'Good' and 'Evil.' Just as the djinn of The Arabian Nights can convert to the True Faith, so can the Other People of Urth come over to the side of the New Sun. The undines claim that they can swim between the stars, which is just what the Hierogrammate Tzadkiel does. This should come as no surprise: devils are just fallen angels, after all.

Goddesses of Urth

Thus, Severian's mother-figures form a trinity of goddesses, each one an aspect of the Great Goddess: Catherine, or Kali, the fiery one, the absent mother; Thecla, or Artemis, the nocturnal huntress, the teacher (a little bit of Athena, here) who becomes the indwelling goddess; and Juturna, the frightful aquatic guide. One could take this further, and consider the nine women with whom Severian is intimate (Thecla's khaibit, Thecla, Dorcas, Jolenta, Cyriaca, Pia, Daria, Valeria, and Gunnie — Apheta in Yesod is not human) as nine muses or aspects of the Great Goddess, or add them to the trinity to form a solar calendar group of twelve goddesses, with Agia as the spurned, unlucky thirteenth member (like Eris/Hecate).

But that would be another essay.

A Timeline of Events (Chart)

Year	Events
70 PS	Autarch Maruthas closes roads (assuming Palaemon is 90 in 1 PS) (I, chap. 12, 102).
67	Reign of Appian. Scandal involving Lomer (28 years old) and Sancha (14 years old). Odilo I serves.
63	Sancha leaves (I assume at 18 years of age) for 50 years.
50	Winnoc born (IV, chap. 12, 74).
40	Dorcas 'dies' giving birth to Ouen, and drowns in lake.
33	Catherine born?

Year	Events
30	Journeyman Palaemon exiled from guild over mysterious scandal (IV, chap 12, 89), whips Winnoc on his way out of Nessus (IV, chap. 12, 74). Old Autarch begins reign, or Appian changes his ways (II, chap 24, 188).
20	(roughly) Thecla born, Severian born, Merryn born, Old Autarch becomes criminal, Catherine in Matachin Tower.
16	Odilo II begins work. (Odilo I served for over 50 years. This compares nicely with St. Odilo, who served for 54 years.)
13	Sancha returns in third year of Odilo II's service.
9	(roughly) Thecla sees Sancha alive (II, chap. 15, 108).
6	Sancha dies at age 75.
1 PS	Events of *The Book of the New Sun*. Lomer is 95. Jader's sister is around 10 years old.
5 SR	Odilo II tells tale of "The Cat."
10	Severian embarks on journey to Yesod. Eata returns from Xanthic Lands.
49	Dux Caesidius dies.
50	Severian returns. Jader's sister 60+. Odilo III serving. Valeria around 70 (V, chap. 43, 302); (V, chap. 44, 313).

(PS = Prior to Severian's reign)
(SR = Severian's Reign)

Bibliography

Campbell, Joseph. *Primitive Mythology,* Viking Penguin, New York, 1987.

Clute, John. *Strokes,* Serconia Press, Washington, 1988 (paperback).

Feeley, Gregory. "The Evidence of Things Not Shown: Family Romance in The Book of the New Sun," *The New York Review of Science Fiction* (#31 and #32), Dragon Press, New York, 1991.

Walker, Barbara G. *The Woman's Encyclopedia of Myths and Secrets,* Harper & Row, 1983.

Wolfe, Gene. *The Shadow of the Torturer,* SFBC edition, 1983.

———. *The Claw of the Conciliator,* SFBC edition, 1983.

———. *The Sword of the Lictor,* SFBC edition, 1983.

———. *The Citadel of the Autarch,* SFBC edition, 1983.

———. *The Urth of the New Sun,* Tor, 1987.

———. *The Castle of the Otter,* SFBC edition, 1983.

****

Afterword for "The Death of Catherine the Weal and Other Stories"

Again the SFBC editions, as among my other early pieces. I only bought the SFBC editions in order to close out my SFBC account. I had joined the SFBC only to get the enigmatic book *The Castle of the Otter.* I had learned about *Castle* in a SFBC ad in a genre magazine. A "Four books for $1" sort of thing.

Prior to that I had no clue about *Castle.* A whole book about The Book?

For that introductory offer I bought four copies of *Castle.* I gave one copy immediately to the Santa Monica Public Library. I do not know if they put it on their shelf or if they sold it right away, but that is what I did.

Once I had created my own Lexicon I naively thought SFBC would be interested in publishing it, and it was already keyed to their edition. That did not work out.

•

A few words about Catherine. Was she even a real Pelerine? Likely she was a prostitute of the House Azure. That would fit clues "exultant" and "khaibit." In that case, if she wore a pelerine cape it was only a costume.

"Perhaps Catherine was not a monial at all, but only a khaibit who escaped the Well of Orchids (or the opening night of the House Azure) while in costume, in the same way that Cyriaca escaped Thrax. An escaped khaibit, impregnated by a commoner, might be enough of a crisis to warrant her stay in the tower" (*Lexicon Urthus, Second Edition,* "Catherine" entry, last paragraph).

Note that Ouen says of Catherine, "She'd run off from some order of monials" (IV, ch. 37, 306). The phrase "some order of monials" shows overlap between the virginal nuns of no fixed location, the quasi-concubines serving the autarch at the Well of Orchids, and the prostitutes serving commoners at the House Azure.

The House Azure is closer to Oldgate, Ouen's home district, than is the Well of Orchids. If a woman left this brothel on opening night, she need only cross the river by boat or bridge, and that is probably the edge of Oldgate.

GENE WOLFE'S NOVELS AND *THE BOOK OF THE LONG SUN*

Inducted into the Science Fiction Museum's Hall of Fame in 2007, Gene Wolfe is an acknowledged master of Science Fiction and Fantasy, renowned for melding literary and genre elements together in his work. His twenty-five novels to date have won him awards and acclaim from around the world: two World Fantasy Awards, one Nebula, one British Science Fiction Award, one British Fantasy Award, two Locus Awards, two SF Chronicle Awards, one John W. Campbell Award, and one Apollo Award.

Gene Wolfe, an only child, was born in Brooklyn, New York, on May 7, 1931. His family moved several times during his childhood, to Illinois, Massachusetts, Ohio, and Iowa. When he was ten they settled down in Houston, Texas, where he attended Edgar Allan Poe Elementary School, and one cannot help but sense that such a literary and fantastic patron left a lasting impression upon him. In college he wrote a couple of stories for a campus magazine, his first experience of being published, but when he dropped out in 1952 he was quickly drafted for the Korean War, where he served in the infantry and saw combat at the front lines. After he was discharged in 1954 he went back to college to complete his degree in Mechanical Engineering. He converted to Catholicism to marry Rosemary Dietsch, and they set up house in Cincinnati, Ohio, where Wolfe worked for Proctor & Gamble as an engineer. He began writing short stories in 1957 and broke into print in 1965, followed by his first novel in 1970. In 1972 Wolfe became editor of the industrial trade magazine *Plant Engineering*, moving with his wife and their four children to Barrington, Illinois. In 1984 Wolfe retired from the magazine in order to write full time.

Early Novels

His first novel, *Operation ARES* (1970), is largely forgotten as an uncharacteristic work that seems more like 1950s-era Heinlein than 1970s-era Wolfe. It is as if Wolfe purposefully adjusted his natural literary esthetic for this book, effectively turning that knob down to zero in order to declare his allegiance to genre. Still, despite this, the novel has some interest for the committed Wolfe fan as it shows elements common to his later work.

Operation ARES gives us a twenty-first century America that has retreated from technology after successfully colonizing Mars. It is a broken welfare state on the verge of collapse. The hero, John Castle, becomes a part of a revolutionary group called "Operation Ares," which is led and supported by invaders from Mars. Their goal is to reestablish technological democracy, and the revolution that follows shows both ideological and military action with a certitude that is quite different from Wolfe's later ambiguity in such matters.

Wolfe's second novel, *Peace* (1975), is a mainstream novel perhaps too subtle. This time it seems as though Wolfe turned his "genre knob" down to zero in order to fully express his literary side. Yet, unlike *Operation ARES*, this novel bears the unmistakable style of Wolfe.

Peace is a memoir of Alden Dennis Weer, born and raised in a quiet Midwestern town. He is an old man and he seems disoriented as he wanders through a large, vacant mansion. On the surface it reads like Kurt Vonnegut's *Slaughterhouse Five* applied to William Faulkner's milieu of dynastic decline: at times Alden appears to be a senile man lost in his own empty house, but at other times he seems to be the last man on Earth. Or perhaps he is a middle-aged man suffering some type of mental breakdown due to loneliness and overwork, a man imagining himself as old and lost.

The Devil in a Forest (1976) is a young adult historical novel with some of the feel of fantasy but not really any of the substance. It tells of Mark, an orphaned peasant in Medieval Europe, a boy who struggles through a somewhat ambiguous landscape of opposing forces: Good and Evil, Christian and Pagan. It is really a mystery novel. As a character, Mark is refreshingly real and modern, rather than being a simple stereotype of a primitive, superstitious peasant.

Thus, these three early novels show the roots of Gene Wolfe's later fiction: the genre conventions of science fiction, fantasy, young adult fiction, and mystery; the techniques of literary fiction; and a deep interest in history, with a belief that people throughout history are equally "modern."

The Urth Cycle

The Book of the New Sun (1980–83) is a masterpiece, that is, a work that shows mastery on the part of the artist. With it, Gene Wolfe suddenly arrived on the scene like a bolt of lightning on a cloudless day. The four volumes of the series collectively won a Nebula Award, a World Fantasy Award, a British Science Fiction Award, two

Locus Awards, a British Fantasy Award, an SF Chronicle Award, an Apollo Award, and a John W. Campbell Memorial Award.

In this science fantasy series, Wolfe reinvents the "dying sun" setting of Clark Ashton Smith's *Zothique* and Jack Vance's *The Dying Earth* by being the first to posit a hero who is willing to meet the gods and win for Earth a new sun to replace the failing one. The Book is a memoir of Severian, supreme ruler of a southern continent of Urth, our Earth in the far future. Severian began life as a torturer, and the strange adventure of how he rose from such a low station to the highest in the land is the main topic of the tale, but along the way there is mystery, ambiguity, and philosophy among the baroque wonder of a fascinating world.

Severian's initial problem is that he falls in love with a female prisoner who has been sentenced to a type of torture that will last for several weeks until she dies. After her initial torture, Severian is unwilling to allow her suffering to continue on, so he breaks the law and allows her a quick death. For this he is banished from the guild, the only home he has ever known.

Winner of an SF Chronicle Award, *The Urth of the New Sun* (1987) is a sequel to The Book that tells of how Severian makes good on his promise by traveling on a starship to the higher universe in order to face the gods and take their test. This relatively simple premise leads to a mind-bending odyssey through time and space.

The Soldier Series

Soldier of the Mist (1986) is a historical fantasy set in ancient Greece around the year 479 B.C. It is the written diary of a mercenary named Latro who has been cursed so that his memory fades away every day. Rather than a memoir, it is a necessary tool for him to review every morning when he wakes up, before he can continue his quest to find out why he was cursed and what he might do to remove the curse. Perhaps as compensation for his condition, Latro has the uncanny ability to see the gods and talk with them. *Soldier of Arete* (1989) finds him traveling north into Macedonia, and the much later, World Fantasy Award winning *Soldier of Sidon* (2006), shows him traveling up the Nile, where he deals with a whole new mythology.

Singletons

Wolfe has written a number of singletons, novels that are not part of a series. He wrote four such works in the late 80s.

Free Live Free (1984) has a salesman, a private detective, a prostitute, and a witch together searching for their missing benefactor, an old man named Ben Free, in a quirky screwball comedy that blends science fiction, gumshoe detective fiction, and the land of Oz, all in the style of a Frank Capra movie.

There Are Doors (1988) opens portals between parallel worlds of alternate Americas, across which Mr. Green searches for his true love, a goddess who might be a woman. In one alternate world, men die after inseminating women, a biological fact that dramatically shapes their culture and civilization.

Castleview (1990) is a strange sort of modern Arthuriana set in the American Midwest. A blend of historical speculation and mythological fantasy in a modern urban setting, a quiet little town named "Castleview" because sometimes a castle mirage appears near the horizon. A new family is moving to town just as phantom knights and other strangeness begin to burst forth.

Pandora by Holly Hollander (1990) is a mystery along the lines of Nancy Drew, famous girl detective. When tragedy strikes close to Holly Hollander, killing a young man, she becomes convinced it was murder, and dedicates herself to solving the case. Set in contemporary Chicago, this novel is the purest expression of the young adult mystery trend that first appeared with *The Devil in a Forest.*

The Solar Cycle

In the 1990s, Wolfe returned to the universe of the New Sun books in order to tell a different story in two linked series, set in a star system far away from that of Urth.

The Book of the Long Sun (1993–96) a four volume series (*Nightside the Long Sun, Lake of the Long Sun, Caldé of the Long Sun,* and *Exodus from the Long Sun*) set on a vast generational starship launched from Urth, long before Severian's birth. The starship is a big cylinder housing an internal world, like a continent on the inside curve of a can. This tube-land is politically divided into isolated city-states, each one following a god or goddess from a pagan pantheon. The hero is a priest named Silk who is enlightened by a different god, the Outsider, and finds he must work with criminals in order to save his neighborhood church.

The Book of the Short Sun (1999–2001) a sequel to **The Book of the Long Sun**, this three volume series (*On Blue's Waters, In Green's Jungles,* and *Return to the Whorl*) is about the two colony worlds, named Blue and Green, settled by the starship dwellers. The story is about Horn, the author and publisher of **The Book of the Long Sun,** and his quest to find Silk, a journey that takes him across several worlds.

The Wizard Knight

The Wizard Knight (2004) is a two-book series, *The Knight* and *The Wizard.* Able, a boy from contemporary America, wakes up in a weird world of chivalric knights, marauding giants, and strange fairy creatures. Able learns how to be a chivalric knight through theory and practice, through hard knocks and failures, as Wolfe applies himself to the Norse mythology and romantic knighthood, once again taking the familiar and rendering it hauntingly alien and vibrant.

"Singleton" or secret companion?

Pirate Freedom (2007) is said to be a singleton, but I consider it to be a companion to **The Wizard Knight**. A dark companion, or shadow, if you will. Again, an American boy is dropped into an alien world. But Christopher is not dropped into an imaginary world of high chivalry; he is stranded in the historical Age of Pirates, a time of raw brutality. Rather than struggling to learn how to be a good knight, Chris must resist becoming the bloody pirate that the times require. All the sanitized and child-safe versions of piracy, from *Treasure Island* to the latest Disney movie, are quickly made to walk the plank. You will never look at pirate fiction the same way again.

Special Focus on **The Book of the Long Sun**

Although it is set in the New Sun universe, the Long Sun series is not in the relatively rare "dying sun" mode of science fantasy. It belongs to the much larger "generation starship" tradition, a subgenre of science fiction that has seen work by Robert A. Heinlein, Harry Harrison, and Brian Aldiss, to name just a few. What really sets it apart from the New Sun books is the style: rather than the baroque form of a decadent, quasi-medieval civilization, the Long Sun is written in the clean prose of an early 20th century Western civilization. Where the New Sun's hero is the dark torturer Severian working his way up, the Long Sun's hero is the sunny priest Silk who is working his way downward.

Silk becomes a detective similar to G. K. Chesterton's Father Brown, and "Father Brown in Space" is an excellent first handle to use, not only for the mystery aspect, but also the style of narration. But Silk is not a Christian priest; he serves an imperial pagan pantheon that uses TV screens to address its worshipers. And he is not a lofty philosopher who never soils his hands; he is a butcher of animal sacrifice who reads their entrails for messages from the gods.

I have been reading Gene Wolfe's work for almost thirty years, and yet I envy you. You are about to read a great work for the first time. It has the intrigue and combat of *Operation ARES,* with some of the ambiguity of *Peace,* and the mystery of *The Devil in a Forest,* all cast in an imagined techno-classical world of historical validity. If you like it enough to read it a second time, you will find that it rewards rereading.

So have fun reading, and should you decide to join the international community of Wolfe fandom, we will welcome you with open arms (and plenty of outrageous theories).

JAPANESE LEXICON FOR THE NEW SUN

In the fall of 1987 I found myself with a new job in a rural town, where one Sunday I visited the local shopping mall, and there in a dump of used paperback books I found a copy of *The Shadow of the Torturer*. It was auspicious, I thought, to find an old friend in a new place, especially since it was a Japanese edition. But then again, I was living in Japan at the time.

To be clear, I couldn't read Japanese very much at all, but I could spot the "Sci Fi" symbol on the book spines (a planet Saturn), and I could read the phonetic writing they use for foreign words and names, such that "Jiin Urufu" is Gene Wolfe.

I opened the book at random. (I should mention that Japanese books are "reverse" to Western standards — their front cover is where our back cover is. In addition to this, the text runs vertically, from top to bottom, from right to left.) So anyway, I opened the book and my eye alighted upon bits of phonetic writing contained within parenthesis — in other words, a parenthetical note on the text. I believe it was a gloss on "amschaspand." (You were guessing it would be "graven." That would have been neat, but no.) I flipped through the book and saw a few others, probably "Nilammon" among them.

"Ah-ha," I thought to myself. "How clever! They have taken notes from Wolfe's article 'Words Weird and Wonderful' in *The Castle of the Otter* and incorporated them as footnotes. I'll bet they don't have any such notes in later volumes."

I bought the book (for 250 yen, about $2 then and now) but didn't search out the others during my two years living there. I brought the book back with me to the States and it remained a curio as I embarked on writing my Lexicon.

Nineteen years later I returned to Japan for a summer job, and it seemed like an opportunity to fill out my set of the Japanese edition, so I did. Contrary to my earlier theory, the other volumes did in fact have word glosses. This meant that it wasn't the easy thing I had thought it was, and that the Japanese translators had, in effect, worked up their own lexicon!

This long-winded and self-aggrandizing introduction is just a prelude to the real thing, the wordlist of the Japanese lexicon for **The Book of the New Sun**. One strategy would be to spread the WWW glosses out among all four volumes, but that does not seem to be the case here — it looks like the translator did most of the work himself, only asking Wolfe directly about two chapters in the fourth volume.

In annotating the words, I trace some to the words defined in the appendix to volume II (marked *), many to "Words Weird and Wonderful" (marked †), and a few to words defined in other articles in *Castle of the Otter* (marked ‡)

Volume I (68 notes)
1. League (measurement) *
2. Exultant †

3. Amschaspand †

4. Arctother †

5. Erebus ‡

6. Matachin tower †

7. Cubit (measurement) *

8. Saros ("period of 6,600 days," i.e., the modern sense of the word. Here the translator made an error, since I believe the ancient sense of the word is required at this spot.)

9. Urth †

10. Cacogen †

11. Chain (measurement) *

12. Minim (measurement) †

13. Half-boot (torture)

14. Ophicleide †

15. Diatryma †

16. Thylacodon †

17. Triskele †

18. Glyptodon †

19. Smilodon †

20. Nilammon

21. Megatherians

22. Graven

23. Drachma

24. Ell (measurement) †

25. Saffron

26. Pantocrator †

27. Hypostases †

28. Quadrille (card game)

29. Urticate †

30. Salpinx †

31. Bordereau †

32. Cabochon emerald †

33. Omophagist †

34. Span (measurement) *

35. Moira †

36. Stride (measurement) *

37. Externs †
38. Ophicleide †
39. Ascians †
40. Baldy
41. Paduasoy †
42. Balmacaan †
43. Surtouts †
44. Dolman †
45. Jerkin †
46. Jelab †
47. Capote †
48. Smock
49. Cymar †
50. Onager †
51. Dulcimer †
52. Lamia †
53. Hesperorn †
54. Oreodont †
55. Cloisonné
56. Fearnought
57. Simar †
58. Succubus †
59. Abacination †
60. Defenestration †
61. Estrapade †
62. Burginot †
63. Verthandi †
64. Coal Sack Nebula
65. Alzabo †
66. Merychip †
67. Teratornis †
68. Pandour †

The article "Words Weird and Wonderful" has around 230 entries for unusual words found in *The Shadow of the Torturer*. The Japanese edition of *The Shadow of the Torturer* gives around 68 glosses. So there are less than a third of those given in "Words Weird and Wonderful."

Volume II (23 notes)

1. Scylla
2. Demiurge
3. Baluchither
4. Kestrel
5. Phorusrhacos
6. Tribade
7. Hierodule
8. Notule
9. Jennet
10. (A note to explain that the White Knight bit mentioned by Jonas in the antechamber is a quote from Lewis Carroll's *Through The Looking Glass.*)
11. Faille (fabric)
12. Naviscaput
13. The three fates
14. Khaibit †
15. Megatherian
16. Capote †
17. Ushas
18. Petasos
19. Tyrian purple
20. Water moccasin (snake)
21. Eclectics (people who fold other cultures into their own — "this refers to Americans"!)
22. Glamour
23. Spelaeae

Volume III (25 notes)

1. Rosolio (wine)
2. Coronas lucis
3. Remontado
4. Sangria (wine)
5. Sanbenito
6. Sikinnis

7. Cuvee (wine)
8. Saros ("18 years," which is about equal to the previous definition of 6,600 days.)
9. Barghest
10. Caloyer
11. (Re: old man in Casdoe's cabin, Palaemon wears glasses.)
12. Notule ("message from Notus, God of South Winds"!)
13. Galleass
14. Gegenschein
15. Squanto
16. Verthandi
17. Amschaspand
18. Xebec
19. (Complication over English word "toadstool," to explain the poisonous, loathsome aspect of something that looks like a yummy *shitake* mushroom.)
20. Pele tower
21. Hellebore
22. Skuld
23. Catamite
24. Logos
25. Estoc

Volume IV (31 notes)
1. Caitanya
2. Bowspirit
3. Narthex
4. Arsinoither
5. Apeiron
6. Schiavoni
7. Bushmaster (snake)
8. Anpiel
9. Merychip
10. Cherkaji
11. Coryphaeus
12. Cuir boli

13. Onager †
14. Phenocod
15. Ophicleide †
16. Ziggurat
17. Calotte (cap)
18. Ransieur
19. Uintathier
20. Platybelodon
21. Acarya (science)
22. Samru (King of Birds)
23. Jupe (female clothing)
24. Aquastor
25. Mandragora
26. Piquenaires
27. Pilani
28. Capote (cape, hood) †
29. Chechia
30. Lugsails
31. Pandour †

A summary of the numbers is in order, which calls for a table. The first column shows the total number of notes per volume, while the second column gives the number of those notes that appear to be from original research rather than being simply copied from *The Castle of the Otter*.

Total: Original
70: 13
23: 21
25: 24
31: 27

Volume I has the lion's share of notes, nearly half of the 149 that is the total, and it also has the lowest percentage of original notes (18%). But in subsequent volumes the percentage of original notes is quite high, so that in the end there are 85 original notes, which amounts to 57% of the 149 total.

In fact I have no certain knowledge that the translator used *The Castle of the Otter* at all, it is just my long-held hunch. He might very well have done all the research on his own.

At the end of Volume IV, the Japanese translator gives three endnotes about a single sentence in chapter 38, specifically about the mysterious séance at the stone town. I'll give the English sentence he is footnoting:

"I know now the identity of the man called Head of Day [1], and why Hildegrin, who was too near, perished when we met [2], and why the witches fled [3]."

Here are his endnotes:

1) "Head of Day" is one of Severian's future shapes.

2) Hildegrin's disappearance was caused by the energy released at the union of old and new Severians.

3) The witch was a member of the temple slaves, and realizing that she had interfered with a very important matter, she withdrew.

In addition, the translator writes that he got help from Gene Wolfe on chapters 37 and 38, and thanks him for that.

•

What is the moral of this story? "Every curio you collect has a deeper meaning that will come to you in the fullness of time"? Maybe.

It is funny, nearly haunting, that I thought the annotations to the Japanese edition of Volume I were a simple work of cribbing notes from "Words Weird and Wonderful," when in fact it is not. I have no doubt that its presence in my collection, or my awareness of its existence, was another obscure milestone on my path to creating a Lexicon. Which is to say, years before *Lexicon Urthus* was even a twinkle in my eye, months before I had even laid eyes upon *The Urth of the New Sun*, my investigative gaze fell upon a narrow spine whose alien, angular letters proclaimed *Jiin Urufu,* so that I caught my breath, smiled, and said, "What have we here?"

WHAT GENE WOLFE EXPECTS OF HIS READERS: *THE URTH OF THE NEW SUN* AS AN ANSWER TO MYSTERIES IN *THE BOOK OF THE NEW SUN*

The Urth of the New Sun (1987) offers the unique opportunity of showing exactly what we are up against in reading (or deciphering) a Gene Wolfe text. This coda to *The Book of the New Sun* (1980-83) answers many mysteries of the original tetralogy, but readers should bear in mind that it was not part of the original plan. In a 1990 essay beguilingly titled "Secrets of the Greeks," Wolfe explains the origins of the fifth book:

> I had an argument with David Hartwell over this last bit [the ending of *The Citadel of the Autarch*]. David felt that I should add one more paragraph saying, Okay, Severian went to the universe next door and borrowed the white hole and fixed the sun and everybody lived happily ever after. I, on the other hand . . . felt that a paragraph wasn't going to be enough. David and I yelled at each other for a while, but eventually came to an agreement. David

would publish *The Citadel of the Autarch* exactly as I had written it, provided that I would write another book in which Severian recounted his trip to the universe next door [i.e., *The Urth of the New Sun*]. (*Castle of Days*, 416–17)

This paper seeks to outline the establishment of four mysteries (two major ones and two minor ones) in TBOTNS and their subsequent solution in *Urth*. I do not claim these are the only mysteries solved, but I believe they provide different models for study.

Major Mysteries

Urth gives clear solutions to a number of major mysteries, including the link between Severian and two other men of widely separated posthistorical periods: the mausoleum builder from the Age of the Autarch (whose funereal bronze looks like Severian) and Apu Punchau from the Age of Myth (who looks like the funereal bronze of the mausoleum builder). In the course of TBOTNS it initially seems that Severian might be the third reincarnation of a man who had started as Apu Punchau and then reincarnated as the mausoleum builder — the cultural belief in reincarnation is established early in the text, when Master Gurloes says, "Doubtless I had acquired merit in a previous life, as I hope I have in this one" (I, chap. 7, 76). By the end of TBOTNS, however, Severian has a new theory of a "First Severian," the original version of himself born in his time, a man who went to Yesod and returned as a time traveler, first building the mausoleum in the Age of the Autarch as a message to his younger self (our narrator Severian), then traveling back to the dawn time to become Apu Punchau, ultimately dying in the time-fight against Hildegrin (II, chap. 31).

In *Urth* both theories are combined and refined, despite the seeming paradoxes. It is plain that Severian will become not only Apu Punchau and the mausoleum builder, but also the Conciliator himself, as well as the New Sun, and even the Sleeper of Ushas. At the same time, Severian is shedding versions of himself, such that he is not, nor will he ever become, the same Apu Punchau who rises from the dead, fights against Hildegrin, and implodes in TBOTNS. This Apu Punchau has a separate life, a different adventure. (Between his rising from the dead and his final implosion, we know of this separate Apu's career as a vivimancer in the stone town, which apparently leads to an encounter with the pelerines at some point, witnessed by his having one of their capes — an artifact he leaves with Severian just before imploding.) So rather than being reincarnations that imply spiritual continuity across linear birth-death cycles, the iterations of Severian are exposed as being time-traveling slivers of himself. Thus Severian becomes like the First Severian in taking actions that affect his younger self, but he remains forever unlike the First Severian in that the First Severian is still shaping him.

Urth also delivers an unambiguous answer to a major mystery that was probably not even recognized as a mystery by most readers — the relation of New Sun and the deluge. In at least seven points in TBOTNS, Severian has intimations of deluge, the most emblematic case being voiced on the ride in a howdah through a stately forest, on the way to meet Vodalus: "I feel now that I'm traveling through the Citadel in a flood, solemnly rowed" (II, chap. 9, 76). *Urth* shows that the arrival of the white fountain in Urth's solar system causes gravity waves to trigger a literal deluge. At the end of his guilt-wracked survey of the destruction, Severian enters the water and re-enacts the vision quoted above:

> Moonlit waves closed about me, and I saw the Citadel below me. Fish as large as ships swam between the towers. . . . this drowned Citadel

vanished like the dream it was, and I found that I was swimming through the gap in the curtain wall and into the real Citadel itself. The tops of its towers thrust above the waves; and Juturna [the undine] sat among them, submerged to the neck, eating fish. (V, chap 48, 341)

With the mysteries laid bare, it becomes apparent that enough clues were provided for such major mysteries to be solved in the original tetralogy. That Severian would travel through time to become both the Conciliator and Apu Punchau, rather than being a reincarnation, avatar, or descendant. And that the world would drown with the coming of the New Sun.

Minor Mysteries

Urth gives answers to minor mysteries of TBOTNS, as well. For example, the memory-free nature of Meschia and Meschiane in Talos' play *Eschatology and Genesis* seems like a playful riff on a collision between the first day in the Garden of Eden and everyday reality.

> *Meschia:* (Examining NOD.) Why, it's only a statue. No wonder he wasn't afraid of it.
> *Meschiane:* It might come to life. I heard something once about raising sons from stones.
> *Meschia:* Once! Why you were only born just now. Yesterday, I think.
> *Meschiane:* Yesterday! I don't remember it . . . I'm such a child, Meschia. I don't remember anything until I walked out into the light and saw you talking to a sunbeam. (II, chap. 24, 213)

The play opens with this comical approach to the end of the world meeting the beginning of the world, where a new Adam and Eve are walking and talking yet are very fuzzy about memories. It isn't until the end of *Urth* that Severian discovers that memory-wiped colonists in fact colonized Ushas:

> I recalled what the young officer had reported [as the Deluge reached the House Absolute]: that Hierodules had landed a man and a woman on the grounds . . . Remembering that, it was simple enough to guess who my priest's forebears had been — the sailors routed by my memories had paid for their defeat with their pasts. (V, chap. 51, 369)

The sailors who had run away from fighting against him at the trial in Yesod are referenced in two brief passages about thirty chapters earlier:

> It seemed that I had no sooner joined the battle than it was over. A few sailors fled from the Chamber; twenty or thirty bodies lay upon the floor or over the benches. (V, chap. 21, 155)

As to their fate, Gunnie asks, "Where are my shipmates? The ones who ran and saved their lives?" and Apheta answers, "They will be returned to the ship" (V, chap. 22, 161).

In this convoluted manner, what seemed a simple joke about Adam and Eve in the play turns out to be entirely true and real.

Then there is the mystery of Hethor's pets. The notule, a monster that is like a dark scrap of flying paper, is small and could easily be carried in a pocket. But the blob-like slug and the man-sized salamander are so big that Severian muses upon a cargo vehicle being necessary:

> But what of [the slug,] the creature we had seen in the hall of testing? . . . A large cart, surely, would have been required to transport and conceal it. Had

Hethor driven such a cart through these mountains?
I could not believe it. (III, chap. 22, 180)

Later, Severian learns from Agia that the monsters
come from magic mirrors (IV, chap. 30, 240). Magic
mirrors, in turn, are introduced to the reader in previous
volumes.

First Severian retells a story Thecla told him about
Domnina's visit to Father Inire's Presence Chamber,
where a Fish was forming at the intersection of eight
magic mirrors. The girl asks him if this is how the
offworlders come to Urth, i.e., by teleportation.

"Has your mother ever taken you riding in her
flier?"
"Of course."
"And you have seen the toy fliers older children
make on the pleasance at night, with paper hulls and
parchment lanterns. What you see here is to the
means used to travel between suns as those toy
fliers are to real ones. Yet we can call up the Fish
with these, and perhaps other things too." (I, chap.
20, 184–85)

Inire's veiled point is that mirrors are used as
propulsive sails, not as a teleportation system between
different stars. But one volume later, Jonas uses the
mirrors in the Presence Chamber to teleport himself away
in the style implied by Domnina's question, albeit to
another universe rather than another star system (II, chap.
18, 167–68).

Magic mirrors are also related, in a somewhat different
way, to *The Book of Mirrors*, which seems to be a
teleportation system from planet Urth to the space near
Tzadkiel's starship (II, chap. 21, 186).

As for the mirrors used on a starship, we have Hethor's
line about "demon-haunted" sails:

Sometimes driven aground by the photon storms,
by the swirling of the galaxies, clockwise and
counterclockwise, ticking with light down the dark
sea-corridors lined with our silver sails, our demon-
haunted mirror sails. (IV, chap. 4, 35)

The implausible cart for Hethor's pets; the Fish in the
Presence Chamber; that the sails of the starship are
mirrors; that the starship sails are haunted by demons; that
Hethor is a former sailor; that the pets have sorcerous
names like "salamander" and "peryton"; etc. From these
scattered points in TBOTNS, the reader was supposed to
have figured out that the old sailor Hethor summons his
pets with a scrap of starship sail cloth, a mirror vastly more
powerful than the "toy" in Father Inire's Presence
Chamber. In *Urth*, Severian travels on the starship and sees
firsthand the magic of the sails in drawing apports into
being. Furthermore, in the fierce fighting on the ship the
sails themselves are damaged, so that Severian is
momentarily frightened of silver scraps flying around,
because they remind him of Hethor's pet notules (V, chap.
15, 106). So we are given evidence of mirror scraps.

(But is it really the case that Hethor uses a bit of
sailcloth to summon his pets? Robert Borski strongly
believes a completely different theory, arguing in chapter
seven of *Solar Labyrinth* [2004] that Hethor is a shape
shifter who enlists the aid of a few other shape shifters. So
Wolfe's mysteries are still open to further analysis and
interpretation — just because I declare a mystery resolved
in a certain way doesn't mean that it doesn't still have
some life to it within the larger critical community. Far
from it! We're all one big, happy family — which is to say,
our numbers aren't very big, we aren't particularly happy,
and we're not at all related.)

In this manner, *Urth* answers many mysteries
established by TBOTNS. Some of the mysteries are
"known mysteries" (for example, the mysterious

connection between Severian, Apu Punchau, and the mausoleum builder), while others are "unknown mysteries" (as in the case of the memory-wiped colonists of Ushas). The exposure of the unknown mysteries in *Urth* causes the text of TBOTNS to open up into unexpected dimensions, rather like a solid cube that suddenly expands into a hyper dimensional tesseract.

•

I close this inquiry with a special note of thanks to David Hartwell, "first reader" of TBOTNS and thus the unelected advocate of all Wolfe readers. Hartwell is a very intelligent man, with a Ph.D. in Comparative Medieval Literature and a taste for difficult texts. He is thus highly qualified, so if *he* doesn't get it, how could we? He served us all very well by arguing with Wolfe about the ending of TBOTNS and then buying its coda, *Urth*. We owe him our sincere gratitude.

Thank you, David Hartwell!

REVIEW OF *NIGHTSIDE THE LONG SUN*

Here it is, the first book of the new **Starcrossers Landfall** series by Gene Wolfe: a fast-paced adventure on a generational starship known by its inhabitants as the 'whorl'; a mystery that starts off with a god-sent vision and ends with an exorcism blending science and religion; and a suspense novel that takes a priest trying to save his gymnasium/church into the underworld of crime.

The hero is a man named Silk, a simple priest who has suddenly been contacted by a god while playing a game that looks to be a cross between basketball and the Aztec ball court game. In a frozen moment Patera Silk receives a vast amount of information from the Outsider, paramount of which is that he himself is the answer to his predecessor's prayers, and that his mission is to save his manteion ('house of prophesy'). Silk goes to the animal market in search of a sacrifice appropriate for this portentous moment, and meets a canny seller who suggests a child is the best sacrifice of all. The grisly specter of human sacrifice serves as an introduction to the lesser but still horrific notion of sacrificing animals that can talk, and Silk eventually purchases such a creature.

Unfortunately, it quickly becomes apparent that the Ayuntamiento (Spanish for 'body of magistrates' or 'municipal government') has just sold Silk's financially strapped manteion to Blood, an underworld figure who deals in an addictive drug called rust. In addition, the sacrifice goes badly, seemingly an ill omen. Desperate, Silk decides to break into Blood's mansion and win back the manteion by reason or force. First he has to find the place, and as the sleeve of night brings darkness to his city of Viron, light to the skylands above, he sets out on his quest.

Nightside introduces a rich new mythology, exotic yet slightly familiar. Mainframe, the realm of the nine gods and fortunate souls, is as visible to the inhabitants of the whorl as Mount Olympus was to the ancient Greeks, and most of the Nine bear a certain resemblance to figures in Greek myth: Pas, sky god with lightning bolts and father of seven gods, seems like Zeus; Echidna, grain goddess and wife of Pas, was a Greek sea monster; Scylla, their eldest child and patroness of Viron, was another sea monster; Tartaros, god of thieves, was a pre-Olympian god who gave his name to the darkest region of Hades; Thelxiepeia the enchanting was one of the Sirens; Phaea the ever feasting, where 'Phaea' (shining one) was a title of Demeter as white sow; Marvelous Molpe seems a female form of 'Molpus' or melody; Hierax the mute might be a masculine form of 'heira,' or priestess; and Sphigx, who is associated with deserts, has a name close to sphinx.

The scenario of the Nine inside the whorl while the long forgotten Outsider breaks through from the void of space seems like a Gnostic response to the cyberpunk cult of the god machine, as well as harkening to Plato's analogy of the cave, where people mistake shadow for substance until one man sees the source of light and the true nature of reality. Probing these gods as false idols, personalities of Urth mortals impressed into the computer when the whorl was created unknown chiliads before, produces some interesting speculation: the Scylla of Mainframe might be the same as the Scylla mentioned in chapter four of *The Claw of the Conciliator* as an enemy of the New Sun; and as the Greek Echidna is married to Typhon, so might two-headed Pas turn out to be the virtual-reality version of the despotic Monarch Typhon who tempted Severian in *The Sword of the Lictor* and imprisoned the Conciliator in *The Urth of the New Sun*.

But this is all background as Silk enlists the help of Auk, a local burglar, and forms a partnership of priest and criminal akin to Chesterton's Father Brown and Flambeau. Auk tries to talk Silk out of his quest, telling him that Blood's mansion is too tough a target even for a professional thief, let alone a complete novice. Silk is adamant, however, and takes to the break-in with all the skill and energy he can muster.

Wolfe is renowned for his use of words weird and wonderful, and *Nightside* is no exception. Although the culture is derived from South America, sprinkled with terms like 'jefe' (boss), 'Juzgado' (court of justice), and 'Alambrera' (wire screen or fire grate), the criminal subculture is patterned on that of Dickens's London, giving the street language of the whorl a heavy dose of thieves' cant. (Among the truly obscure words in *Nightside* is 'azoth,' an alchemical term for mercury, which was also applied to the principle of the immaterial.) With third-person narration, the action is immediate, the outcome is uncertain, and *Nightside the Long Sun* begins with a bang what promises to be a great new series of four books.

REVIEW OF *IN GREEN'S JUNGLES*

It is my great pleasure to herald the arrival of a new masterpiece from Gene Wolfe: *In Green's Jungles,* the second volume of *The Book of the Short Sun* trilogy. This represents a new level: It may be the best thing he has ever written.

When we last saw Horn, the hero/narrator of *On Blue's Waters,* he had left the city of Gaon under cover of darkness and was making his way northwest toward his home city of New Viron. As *Green* begins we find him in a new town where he quickly receives a new name, "Incanto," and becomes deeply involved in local conflicts, all resulting in something like a Spaghetti Western told by Scheherazade.

The town's name is Blanko. It is one of four colonies (Blanko, Soldo, Olmo, Novella Citta) in close proximity to each other on Blue, all founded by settlers from the same city (Grandecitta on the *Whorl*). Blanko's trouble is Duko Rigoglio, leader of Soldo and the man who would be king of the four colonies.

Horn is invited to dine at the farmhouse of Inclito, the *de facto* leader of Blanko. On the way there, Inclito tells Horn that he fears there is a spy within his household and asks him to discover who it is. (Could it be the cook, the maid, the scullery maid, the coachman, either of the two hired farm hands, the daughter, the daughter's friend, or the grandmother?) So against a backdrop of looming warfare we enter a country estate mystery . . . and at the dinner table we have a story-telling contest among the diners.

Horn began *The Book of the Short Sun* intending to tell the story of his failed quest to find the hero Silk, protagonist of *The Book of the Long Sun*, and bring him back to the planet Blue. In *Blue* we learn he had set out from Blue, was sidetracked into a trip to Green (the inhumi planet), somehow went from Green to the *Whorl* (the orbiting generation starship where Silk was last seen). On the *Whorl* he met with failure of some sort, then was forced to leave in a lander that took him to Blue, compelled by the same people who then installed him as their leader in Gaon. This quest from Blue to Green to *Whorl* and back to Blue seems to have taken about a year; the writing of *Blue* took about a year.

Blue followed this plan and reads like a version of *The Odyssey* where Odysseus begins telling his own story not as a stranger in the court of King Alcinous, but as a newly installed Rajan of Gaon. The report of his earlier seaborne adventure is the main narrative thrust, while the incidental journal notes of his situation while writing the report show him administering his new kingdom. This narrative device is somewhat similar to that used by Wolfe in *The Soldier of the Mist:* part narrative, part journal, all begun *in medias res* and told in "real time." But where Latro's memory problems make the Soldier books a choppy and challenging text, the narrative flow of *The Book of the Short Sun* is as smooth, as smooth as . . . dare I say it? . . . Silk.

People in the narrative present keep mistaking Horn for Silk, even when they only know of Silk from reading *The Book of the Long Sun,* which was written by Horn. As a grown man, Horn had been given the quixotic task of making manifest a hero from a book written from a boy's viewpoint. It is hard to be a hero; in Horn's case it is perhaps even harder to find a hero; but here the biographer has somehow become so similar to his subject that people meeting him see the hero and not the author.

In Green's Jungles is very much about stories and storytellers. The story Horn is trying to tell shifts on him with *Green:* the focus moves away from his past failures on Green and into new challenges on Blue. The story is changing on Horn in the present, in part because what he thought of as a completed action was in reality only the middle of one. The old story continues in diminished form, with herculean labors and nightmarish visions "in Green's jungles." The story is changing Horn himself; Horn is changing the story. Many riddles from *Blue* are resolved, such as why Horn looks so much like Silk, how Horn traveled from Green to the *Whorl,* and exactly how close Blue and Green are during conjunction.

The new story is about fathers and daughters, in the same way that *Blue* was about fathers and sons. This is very new for Horn, because he has raised three sons, but no daughters. He learns through interactions between Inclito and his daughter Mora; through his own interactions with Mora and her girlfriend Fava; and then there is Jahlee, an inhuma vampire who grows nearly as close to Horn as the inhumu Krait, who calls himself Horn's son, did in *Blue*.

The world of Blue is a mess. The crops are failing, wars of conquest are breaking out, slavery has emerged (the new details on how slavery came to Blue provide a powerful and complex situation). Conjunction with Green means that a fresh wave of inhumi have arrived to prey upon the colonists; Horn's relations with the vampires becomes ever more complex (he made deals with a few in order to win the war for Gaon in *Blue*, but by the end of that book they were stalking him).

But there are strange signs that give hope. Horn's education by the enigmatic Vanished Ones, the centaur like creatures who previously inhabited Blue, continues and he gains new powers. And his dealings with inhumi are awakening in him an unpredictable magic. Things are building toward a spectacular climax, and I look forward to the next volume.

REVIEW OF *STRANGE TRAVELERS*

Here is a brand new collection of fifteen stories. Originally published in magazines, theme anthologies, and a program guide, they offer a wide variety of styles and modes for your reading and re-reading pleasures. Since this is a review, I'm going to fly through the list of stories so you can see what is there, learn what you remember, and wonder at what you are missing.

"Bluesberry Jam" (1996) is set in a permanent traffic jam, where a talented young street musician wanders away from the family car, in search of love and music. (Reminds me of Delany, especially the young musician heroes of *The Einstein Intersection* and *Nova.*) What begins as a straight "Orpheus" quest becomes caught up in the nature of two different types of musician: the self-taught, intuitive kind, who make up new songs in and of the present; and the highly polished "schooled" type, who perform the old hits from distant times and lands, with no personal input beyond the performance. And then it becomes something else again.

"One-Two-Three For Me" (1996) is a ghost story at an archaeological dig in the distant future.

"Counting Cats in Zanzibar" (1996) has a woman with

seven pseudonyms being pursued by her past: the robots she helped create. (New Wave-ish, as if Ballard did a downbeat version of Asimov's robopsychologist heroine Susan Calvin: something we might call "Eurydice in the Robot Kingdom"?)

"The Death of Koshchai the Deathless" (1995) is a tale of Old Russia, inspired by the tale of the same name told by Andrew Lang in *The Red Fairy Book*. A blend of (very funny) comical and horrific elements.

"No Planets Strike" (1997) is told by a donkey on an alien world inhabited by cruel, fairy-like beings. It could very well be set in Briah, the same universe as *The Book of the (New/Long/Short) Sun.* (The title is from "Hamlet.")

"Bed And Breakfast" (1995) is about a man and a woman who meet at an inn close to hell. Almost hard-boiled, a sort of "supernatural realism" that reminds me of Chesterton and C. S. Lewis at their best.

"To the Seventh" (1996) describes a chess game between God and the Devil, which translates into galactic warfare on the smaller scale. Space Opera.

"Queen of the Night" (1994) gives us a boy raised by ghouls until he comes to the attention of the Queen of the Night herself and trades one world for another. Erotic Horror.

"And When They Appear" (1993) is a very sobering Christmas story, with a boy in an automated house. (Makes me think again of Ballard: imagine *Empire of the Sun* crossed with Bradbury's "There Will Come Soft Rains" in *The Martian Chronicles*.)

"Flash Company" (1997) has a man being tutored in the ways of love by a haunted player piano.

"The Haunted Boardinghouse" (1990) is located in a neo-Victorian Illinois, a few centuries in the future. A young classics scholar is invited to be the new librarian at a school in a strange town that played a pivotal role in a war against Mexican invaders several generations before. (The building of the title is highly reminiscent of the house in

John Crowley's *Little, Big,* and the story begins as a low-tech world-renewed, the sort of agrarian arcadia beloved by both survivalists and ecotopians.)

"Useful Phrases" (1992) could fit in with Wolfe's earlier *Bibliomen,* since it concerns a book dealer who becomes obsessed with a primer of an imaginary language and the world it seems to describe. Clearly related to Borges' famed "Tlon, Uqbar, Orbis Tertius."

"The Man in the Pepper Mill" (1996) has a boy exploring a magical world that intersects our own through the dollhouse of his dead sister. He is also trying to find a man to marry his mother and be his stepfather.

"The Ziggurat" (1995): a mountain cabin, a messy divorce-in-progress, a suicidal engineer, the promise of child custody battles, a sudden snowstorm, an alien invasion. A horror story.

"Ain't You 'Most Done?" (1996) features a successful businessman whose secret dream is to be a professional musician. He is caught in a traffic jam that seems to last forever . . .

Because the last story links directly back into the first story, I find myself pondering over how the other stories might connect to each other: Quixote Complex ("enamored of other worlds found in books") forms a link between "The Haunted Boardinghouse" and "Useful Phrases" (both also have foreign phrases as their keystones); the fates of the boys in "Queen of the Night" and "And When They Appear" might link the stories as being similar; the haunted artifacts of "One-Two-Three For Me" and "Flash Company" show them as contrasts. As far as themes go, the struggle between men and women in the name of love seems to be present in nearly all the stories. Couples in various permutations (pursuit, courtship, consummation, estrangement) dot the landscape rather like they do in Ovid's *Metamorphoses.*

Many of the stories seem to have a reinvigorated "New Wave" aesthetic: I have mentioned Delany and Ballard (twice), but there are also three stories that seem linked to James Tiptree, Jr.: "Counting Cats in Zanzibar," "The Ziggurat," and "The Man in the Peppermill" (which mentions Tiptree directly). Technology is bad; a post-technological world is a pastoral utopia; stories are downbeat (situations go from bad to worse; problems can hardly be identified, let alone "solved"; characters suffer depression, suicidal impulses, paranoia, etc., and do not get better; etc.); sexual relations are free but pointless when not actually destructive.

Is this a collection of homages and near-pastiches? After all, in the past Gene Wolfe has given us such gems as "Our Neighbor by David Copperfield" (Dickens), "Remembrance to Come" and "Suzanne Delage" (Proust), "The Rubber Bend" and "Slaves of Silver" (Arthur Conan Doyle), among others. And in talking about *Strange Travelers* with other readers, a few people have mentioned that "One-Two-Three For Me" is very much like a classic horror story by M. R. James ("Oh Whistle, and I'll Come to You, My Lad").

This line of speculation (i.e., "is this story original or based on something else?") of course links back to the two types of artist depicted in "Bluesberry Jam." And where there is jam, we must have toast. So I propose this one: "To Gene Wolfe, for providing such a smorgasbord of food for thought. Cheers!"

(What? My editor gestures from down the table . . . I am far under word-count, he wants more . . . all this while he reads *The Dying Earth* for the first time! Well, that's certainly important, better late than never. Toss back this glass of wine, pour myself another.)

Oo-kay. Now I will do a bit of work on one of the stories, "The Haunted Boardinghouse" — I will carve the roast, as it were.

As I mentioned before, the building seems inspired by John Crowley's *Little, Big,* in which a rambling house with five faces serves as the axis for the family saga. Each face of Crowley's house is done in a different architectural style (but he is a bit sneaky about revealing what the fifth one is; there's a slight paradox involved) and there are hints in *Little, Big* that each face matches up to a different season (again, slightly odd since we moderns usually count four seasons).

Wolfe's house has four faces, and we know what the styles are, and even most of the street names:

Style: Neo-Classical
Street: Water
Note: boy climbing out window (p. 229)

Style: Tudor
Street: (not given)
Note: window of Enan's room (p. 230)

Style: Neo-Victorian
Street: Prescott
Note: "your world is neo-Victorian" (p. 230)

Style: Contemporary
Street: Gate
Note: (p. 230)

The haunting details about the boy who fell out the window, took years to die of the injuries sustained, and continues to climb out the window: this points to the time warping nature of the architecture. It may also be that the boy in question is none other than Wade, the student who befriends Enan.

In addition, rather than being (possibly) related to seasons, each face seems linked to its appropriate time point in history: since the story clearly ends with Enan going off across time and space to save Rome from Hannibal, the Neo-classical face leads to there; and since we are told that Enan comes from a neo-Victorian world, then that is the face that leads to Enan's world. Finally, the miraculous saving of Rome from Hannibal is matched by the saving of Granville from the Mexicans, thus the link to the Contemporary face is made plain. So these time-travelers go to the lands they are most enamored of, at the time when they are most needed.

But wait, I have only traced out three of the faces. Is the Tudor face another recruiting station, like the Neo-Victorian face, with no associated "miraculous" save from invasion? Maybe it is. Maybe it isn't.

Architecture: Invasion
Neo-classical: Hannibal's attempted invasion of Rome
Tudor: Spanish Armada's attempted invasion of England
Neo-Victorian: (recruiting station for Enan and Wade)
Contemporary: Mexico's attempted invasion of Granville

What makes me think of the defeat of the Spanish Armada (aside from another spoiled invasion that ranks up there with the Mongols failing to take Japan) is the fact that the defense of Granville involved a lot of boats on the river (p. 214), and the big ships of the Armada were done in by a lot of smaller, more nimble craft.

A final Crowley note: the mystery of the two Mrs. Seelys has a slight parallel in *Little, Big* but a much more pronounced one in Crowley's *Ægypt* books.

Anyway, one of the surprises in my reading of this story is this: just as Rome was nearly wiped out in relative infancy, yet then went on to undreamed of glory and accomplishment of the Roman Empire; (and perhaps England, too, narrowly missed being crushed and delivered the English Renaissance and its avatar William Shakespeare;) so has Granville been spared . . . strongly suggesting that all of America's true greatness still lies before it in Enan's non-technological, neo-Victorian period (rather than behind it, as we might expect in such a post-technological setting).

Okay, that's it. I'm done, I'm outta here. Enjoy your meal!

REVIEW OF *SHADOWS OF THE NEW SUN*

I avoid writing reviews because it only leads to writing more reviews. Despite this adamantine fortress, my opinion on the Gene Wolfe tribute anthology *Shadows of the New Sun* (2013) was sought out by the curious, and thus I find myself here, bending my rule for vanity, even in a case where I should recuse myself. So, here is not a review.

To begin with the obvious, I am an unreliable reader. You already know what I am going to say about this book, so let's just get it out of the way: Buy it, read it with joy, give copies as presents.

With that done, I now embark into the weeds, the details, the "behind the scenes." It is a journey across much time and little space.

I remember very well when the concept of a Gene Wolfe tribute anthology first appeared to me, but the second time was a few years later. It was sometime in the mid-1990s, at a house in Berkeley. There were fissures in the backyard.

I was sharing an afternoon with my two favorite poets, Andrew Joron and Robert Frasier, at Andrew's house. We were in the kitchen, away from the hypnotic fissures whispering their thirst for blood. Over a bottle of wine — white, I believe, but that doesn't make sense since Andrew is a stickler for red — we were discussing Gene Wolfe, mainly because my poetry acumen is quite limited. (You will recall that Robert interviewed Gene Wolfe in the 1980s, for the fanzine *Thrust*.) We spoke of Gene's poetry, his 1978 Rhysling Award, and then I suppose under the unspoken topic of "What would Michael publish next?" Robert floated the thought-balloon of a tribute anthology.

I groaned, I sighed, I rolled my eyes. We discussed three angles of the prospective project: the good (the celebration of an author); the challenge (selecting among a spectrum from "homage" to "pastiche," while avoiding the lowest grade fan fiction); and the work (how to find and recruit the biggest names possible, in addition to the usual small press troubles). On the one hand it seemed the quintessential small press project, a work of concentrated, dedicated love, realistically limited to a print run of 500 copies; but in the next sip of Riesling the idea looked so difficult as to be effectively, quixotically, *Sisyphusianly* impossible, a project for a mainstream publisher, and there seemed faint likelihood of that coming to pass.

In short, I admit I had dreamed of such a book — more accurately, others had independently spoken to me of the notion, and I had repeatedly refused to do it myself. Instead I chased after such projects as a hardcover edition of *The Island of Doctor Death and Other Stories and Other Stories,* two collections of uncollected stories, *et cetera.*

None of those were published. The tribute anthology, though, is here.

Let's start with that title, *Shadows of the New Sun.* It is a good one — so good, in fact, that it had already been used for Peter Wright's 2007 book of essays and articles by and about Gene Wolfe (including, I must add, Robert Frasier's aforementioned interview). Obviously, such a titling is a Wolfean thing to do. Acknowledging this, it is with some sorrow I admit having advised Robert Borski not to title his first book "The Naked Sun," because that was the title of Asimov's 1957 robot novel. (He went with *Solar Labyrinth.*) If he had gone ahead with his first choice, he might have quite logically titled his next book, the one about the Long Sun and the Short Sun, "The Caves of Steel." (He went with *The Long and the Short of It.*) Still, the case in question is another twist again, a loop-the-lupine loop (tip of the hat to Philip José Farmer), to name a Wolfe tribute anthology after a Wolfe-studies collection, such that any confusion results in more Wolfe-related sales, rather than sales of Asimov, Mark Twain (*Innocents Aboard* ≠ *Innocents Abroad*), or Nabokov (*The Laughter at Night* ≠ *Laughter in the Dark*).

This tribute anthology confirms what I thought before, when poets and Rhône wine sharpened my mind, and yet it also manages to avoid all the pitfalls. It achieves the difficult task of providing the virtues of both the small press and the big press, in effect forging an alchemical wedding. It has mainly big name authors, as befits a big press production, but I was pleasantly surprised by the intensity of feeling coming through in these stories. Nobody here is "phoning it in," and at times the emotions on display made me feel as though I were reading private, personal letters. Kudos to the writers, and kudos to the editors! Even with all the resources at their fingertips, they still could have produced a mediocre tome, but they did not — they succeeded in wonderful triumph.

From my perspective, that should be the best outcome, right? Being able to enjoy a top-rate product without having had to go through all the blood, sweat, and tears of producing it.

Gene Wolfe himself has two stories in the book, which makes him both the honored guest and the waiter, or something. The course of reading through the story sequence has a compounding effect upon me, the echoing and reactive nature of the stories in *The Arabian Nights,* or better, *The Canterbury Tales,* where each narrator is a separate individual united to the others by threads of common interest. Here it is as if eighteen writers sat together around a table, each telling a tale in turn, and though each had arrived by a separate path, still there were the similar sights they had seen and the strangest coincidences. In all, a shared meal of nineteen courses.

But I get ahead of myself. While I will not comment on every one of the stories, I must start with the first story, or the story of the first story, and my reason to recuse myself. It is a bitter tale.

The first story is "Frostfree" by Gene Wolfe, about a fembot sent from the future on a mission. I was intimately involved in its writing, a project that began in 2009 when I was approached by a group of Wolfe fans whom I knew from the Internet. They wanted to commission an original short story from Gene Wolfe for inclusion in a small print-run book. I was skeptical, but I mentioned it to Gene and he said he was amiable if I hammered out all the details first. I hammered and I hammered, and it all seemed right. Then, as per the agreement with Gene, I pestered and I pestered him to write the thing on time, and he did. The story itself seemed to be partially inspired by a Tee-shirt Gene had seen me wearing in Seattle one day in 2007. This shirt is a unique artifact I had made myself, grabbing an anime image from a favorite Japanese cartoon and adding to it the words "Combat Waitress ... From the Future!" (For my musings on such cartoons, please see my latest Kindle e-book, *True SF Anime.*)

After all those months, problems arose with the publisher and Gene had to withdraw his story from the project. I hope he has forgiven me. (And I hope that other enterprising fans — the graphic novelist in San Francisco, the game designer in France — will forgive me for not helping them more.)

The anthology's second story is from Neil Gaiman. I first knew Neil Gaiman as a Wolfe fan in the early 1990s where I saw him write on the topic on the GEnie board. He had interviewed Gene at Fantasycon 1983, his first chance to meet his hero. Neil Gaiman is a genial person but I bungled my way into offending him on the topic of comic book studies — my follow-up expansion, never given, was that I felt the English department did not have the visual arts vocabulary to deal with anything other than text; even the typographical antics of *Tristram Shandy* push the limits. Comic book art requires art studies and cinema studies, it seems to me. I hope Neil Gaiman has forgotten the incident, or, even better, forgiven me.

I did not meet Neil Gaiman at World Fantasy Con in Tucson 1991, even though we were both there. That was where he won an award for *Sandman,* and saw a shooting star that inspired him to write *Stardust*; whereas I met Gene Wolfe in person for the first time, and together we tried to pressure David Hartwell into buying my lexicon project, one (big press) way or the other (small press) way. No dice!

In 2012 Neil Gaiman did me the honor of introducing himself to me at the Chicago Literary Hall of Fame event celebrating Gene Wolfe. He said that I was "fan number one." That is flattering, or unsettling, or both — who, then, are these other fans, who know so much more than I do? Who is "fan zero," and "fan minus one"? Who are the secret masters, wise enough to go unnamed?

At that same event I renewed acquaintances with Michael Swanwick, who provides the ninth story in the tribute anthology. I had first met him at World Fantasy Con in Baltimore 1995, where Dan Knight, small press publisher of *Young Wolfe* (1992) and *Letters Home* (1991), introduced him to me as a Gene Wolfe fan. At the fabulous mansion of coin-operated machines and vast musical organs, I spoke with Michael Swanwick about the recent *John Carter* (2012) movie, happy to find that he enjoyed it nearly as much as I. He said green Martians were based on American blacks, and I was about to argue with him on that point but then the show was starting and I had to shut up and find a chair. So here is what I was going to say — Hadn't it already been established in print that the green Martians were based upon Arabs? I believe that is the case, and John Carter's uniting of the tribe is a lot like that action by Lawrence of Arabia … except that John Carter did it first, which is boggling. Was T. E. Lawrence inspired by Barsoom?

I was involved in the production of a second story in the anthology, a third reason to recuse myself, but the most pleasant of them. In 2012 William Dietz contacted me by email to sound out ideas for a New Sun story. I was delighted to offer what assistance I could. He had a few scenarios, and we developed one. The result is "In the Shadow of the Gate." (If he gets a future commission to write a novel set in the *Fallout*-franchise, I hope he remembers my offer to help out with any lore questions he might have!) I had the pleasure of meeting William Dietz in person at Nebula Weekend in San Jose 2013, the event where Gene Wolfe received a Grand Master Award.

Also on hand in San Jose was Marc Aramini, another contributor to the anthology. I know Marc from the Internet Gene Wolfe community, and I have met him in person a couple of times. His story, which is his first published fiction as far as I can tell, should give pride to the fan community, since it is high quality work, sharing the venue with best sellers. Marc is, among his many other talents, a boxer, as Gene Wolfe told the audience back at the coin-operated mansion in 2012. (Marc and I were sitting up in the balcony, along with James Wynn, another fan who should write more.) This detail came to my mind as I read the fist-fighting details in Gene's latest novel, *The Land Across* (2013). Granted that Gene had boxing experience in his youth, but still I sense the influence of Marc here.

So there you have it, a collection of stories. It is tempting for me to say there's a this-genre story and a that-genre story, but I don't want to ruin the surprise. Nor do I want to list all the story linkages, for the same reason, or a very similar one. Instead I'll end with a timeline.

1978: Gene Wolfe wins Rhysling Award.

1981: Michael first reads Gene Wolfe work.

1982: Robert Frasier interviews Gene Wolfe.

1983: Neil Gaiman interviews Gene Wolfe.

1991: WFC Tucson; *Letters Home* published.

1992: *Young Wolfe* published.

1995: Robert Frasier talks about Wolfe tribute; WFC Baltimore.

2004: Robert Borski's *Solar Labyrinth* published.

2006: Robert Borski's *The Long and the Short of It* published.

2007: Gene Wolfe inducted into the Science Fiction Hall of Fame, Seattle; Peter Wright's *Shadows of the New Sun* published.

2009: The "Frostfree" fiasco.

2012: Gene Wolfe wins Fuller Award, Chicago.

2013: Gene Wolfe wins Grand Master Award, San Jose; *The Land Across* published.

2014: Michael's *True SF Anime* e-book published.

ABOUT THE AUTHOR

Michael Andre-Driussi has written a number of science fiction reference books, from *Lexicon Urthus* (1994) to *Handbook of Vance Space* (2014). With Alice K. Turner he co-edited *Snake's-hands: the Fiction of John Crowley* (2001). His fiction, published in venues from *Aberrations* to *Wicked Words Quarterly*, has been collected in *Fallout Stories* (2016), *Doomsday and Other Tours* (2016), and *The Jizmatic Trilogy* (2017).

Printed in the USA
CPSIA information can be obtained
at www.ICGtesting.com
LVHW101002281223
767564LV00004B/646